M.C. Beaton

Agatha Raisin *and the*

BUSY BODY

Constable • London

CONSTABLE

First published in the USA in 2010 by St Martin's Press,
175 Fifth Avenue, New York, NY 10010

First published in the UK in 2010, by Constable,
an imprint of Constable & Robinson Ltd

Paperback edition published in the UK in 2011 by Robinson,
an imprint of Constable & Robinson Ltd

This edition published in 2016 by Constable

3 5 7 9 10 8 6 4

A CIP catalogue record for this book
is available from the British Library.

ISBN: 978-1-47212-145-5

Typeset in Palatino by Photoprint, Torquay
Printed and bound by CPI Group (UK) Ltd, Croydon, CR0 4YY

Papers used by Constable are from well-managed forests and other
responsible sources.

Chapter One

Having found that her love for her ex-husband, James Lacey, had more or less disappeared, Agatha Raisin, middle-aged owner of a detective agency in the English Cotswolds, decided to hit another obsession on the head.

For the past two years she had been determined to create the perfect Christmas, the full Dickensian dream, with disappointing results. So she decided to flee Christmas by taking a long holiday in Corsica. Her second in command, young Toni Gilmour, was more than capable of dealing with the usual run of dreary divorce cases and missing pets, the bread and butter of the agency.

Agatha had booked a room in a hotel in the town of Porto-Vecchio at the south of the Mediterranean island. She had googled the information and found that it was an old Genoese town with a winter temperature in the low sixties Fahrenheit.

She arrived at the hotel late because it took her over an hour to find a taxi at Figari Airport. Agatha looked forward to celebrating Christmas with a lobster dinner. No more turkey.

The receptionist at the hotel greeted her with, 'I see you've booked in with us for three weeks. Why?'

Agatha blinked. 'Why? I'm on holiday.'

'But what are you going to do?' asked the receptionist. 'Most of the shops and restaurants are closed. You don't have a car. There aren't that many taxis, and the ones that there are don't like short trips.'

'I'll think about it,' said Agatha wearily. 'I'm hungry. Do you have a restaurant?'

'No, but if you go out of the hotel and turn right and then next left it will take you up to the citadel and there are a few restaurants there.'

Agatha left her luggage and set off on the steep climb up to the citadel. The Christmas decorations were the most beautiful she had ever seen but the streets were deserted. She reached the square in the centre of the old citadel. There were two restaurants open and, in the middle of the square, an empty skating rink where men were pouring water on the surface of the ice so that it would freeze overnight. Agatha's spirits sank even lower. She had not imagined Corsica ever getting cold enough for ice to freeze.

There was a heated area for smokers facing one restaurant. She sat down and ordered a meal, which turned out to be nothing special and came to forty-two euros, which, thanks to the falling sterling, meant it cost her the equivalent of forty-two pounds.

She sat and puffed on a cigarette and debated whether to hire a car or not. The trouble was Agatha could not parallel park. In fact, she only felt happy when there was an empty parking space that could take the size of a truck. The cars she had seen parked were all tight together. How on earth did they manage to get out without damaging the cars parked up against them, front and back?

Agatha did not want to admit failure. She did not want to return home and say she had made a mistake. A good night's sleep was all she needed. She trudged back to the hotel through the deserted streets under the sparkling golden haloes of Christmas decorations around every street lamp.

The next day was sunny. After a good breakfast, Agatha asked directions to the port, where she was sure there must be delicious seafood. 'There's a quick way down from the citadel,' said the receptionist, 'but it's terribly steep.' Agatha's arthritic hip gave a nasty twinge.

'What about round by the road?' she asked. 'How long would that take?'

'About half an hour.'

So Agatha set out. And walked and walked and walked until, an hour and a half later, she found herself at the port. There was a restaurant open, but no lobster. She ordered a salmon steak, the special of the day, reflecting that she could easily have got the same thing back home in England. At the end of the meal, she hopefully asked the waitress to phone for a taxi. But the result was no taxi would take her. 'They only like long trips from town to town,' said the waitress.

So Agatha decided to try the shortcut up to the citadel. It was incredibly steep. At one point, she could have sworn the pavement was staring her in the face. The pain in her hip was severe and she panted for breath the whole way up. When she reached the square in the citadel, she sank down into a chair in a restaurant and ordered a beer. She took out a packet of cigarettes and then put them away again. She was still gasping from the climb up.

I have to get out of here, she thought. Bonifacio is supposed to be beautiful. Dammit. I'll hire a car and go there. There's bound to be lobster there.

Back at the hotel, she checked Bonifacio on her laptop. She read that the harbour was exclusive and sophisticated with many good restaurants. There was an old medieval town on the cliff above the harbour. There did not seem to be many hotels open but she found one that looked promising and booked a room, saying cautiously she did not know how long she would be staying.

As she drove off at dawn the following morning in her rented car, she was glad of the deserted roads and the fact that the route to Bonifacio was well signposted. As the sun rose on another perfect day and her car climbed up into the mountains, Agatha felt happy. It was all going to be all right.

The hotel turned out to be outside the town. She was given a small house in the grounds of the hotel, like a fairy-tale house, made of old stone with a red-tiled roof. There was a large living room, bedroom and a bathroom with an enormous bath. The hotel only served dinner, so, once unpacked, Agatha drove down to the port.

Practically all the restaurants were closed. In the short time since her arrival, the sky had darkened and a freezing wind was bending the palm trees in the port and singing in the shrouds of the yachts moored alongside the quay. Agatha had lunch in one of the few restaurants. The food was good – but no lobster. Determined to visit the old town, after lunch Agatha drove up into it and found herself in a terrifying maze of very narrow streets. Several times she nearly scraped the car. Several times she nearly lost her way, before, with a sigh of relief, finally finding the route to the port again. Rain was slashing against the windscreen.

'Sod this for a game of soldiers,' Agatha howled to the uncaring elements. 'I'm going home.'

By the time she got to Charles de Gaulle, she had a sore throat and was cursing that she now had to leave by terminal 2E instead of the former 2F. The terminal was huge and bewildering and the check-in chaotic. The only bright spot was when the man checking her bags through security asked to see her passport. He studied her photograph. 'This, madame,' he said, 'is the photograph of a beautiful woman, and you are even more beautiful today.'

Agatha, accustomed to the French ability to flirt, answered, 'Monsieur, such a compliment coming from a handsome man like yourself makes me feel beautiful.' He smiled, everyone in security smiled, and Agatha felt a glow. Aren't the French marvellous when it comes to flirting, she thought. It's a technique we lost in Britain as soon as the birth-control pill arrived on the scene. Flirt with a man back home and all you get is: enough of this nonsense, drop your drawers.

The gate for the flight to Birmingham was down in the basement. Then all the passengers were put on a bus that took so long to reach the plane that Agatha wondered whether they were going all the way to Calais.

As she drove down the road leading to Carsely, towards her cottage, she thought, I can ignore Christmas here just as well as I could in Corsica. But Agatha automatically looked for the Christmas tree on top of the church tower. No Christmas tree. She blinked in surprise. Every year, the lights of the Carsely Christmas tree on top of the square church tower had shone out over the surrounding landscape. She circled the village green. Even the second Christmas tree, which usually stood there in December, was missing, as were the fairy lights, usually strung across the main street of the village.

Agatha mentally shrugged. They had probably come to their senses and were all fed up with all the commercial hoo-ha of Christmas. Still, the church could hardly be accused of being commercial. She did not know then that there was only one man behind the darkness, one man who was going to bring death and fear into the Cotswolds.

It had all started the day after she had left for Corsica. The vicar, Alf Bloxby, with two sturdy helpers, was mounting the steep stairs to the church roof, carrying a Christmas tree. Once up on the top of the tower, they were just looking out the cables kept in a chest on the

6

tower roof to anchor the tree, when a voice from the doorway to the tower cried, 'Stop!'

Alf turned round in surprise. Standing in the doorway was Mr John Sunday, an officer with the Health and Safety Board based in Mircester.

'You can't put that tree up,' he said. 'It's a danger to the public. It could fall off the tower and kill someone.'

Mr Sunday was a small, barrel-chested man with a pugnacious face and thick pepper-and-salt hair. 'I am within my rights as an officer of the Mircester Health and Safety Board,' he said. 'If you persist in erecting that tree, I will have you taken to court. Furthermore I am putting red tape round the gravestones in the churchyard.'

'Why on earth?' exclaimed Alf.

'Because they might fall over.'

'Look here, you stupid man, those gravestones have been standing for hundreds of years without falling over.'

'A gravestone fell over in a cemetery in Yorkshire and injured someone. It is my job to ensure safety.'

'Oh, go away,' said Alf wearily. 'Come on, men. Let's get this tree up.'

But two days later the vicar received an official letter from the Health and Safety Board telling him he must take down the tree or face court proceedings.

The Carsely parish council was then informed that if they wished to put up fairy lights along the main street, they were not to use ladders. A cherry picker had to be

7

used instead by two trained workers, which would have cost the village one thousand two hundred pounds in training fees, plus their wages and the cost of the equipment. Every light fitting must undergo a 'pull test' using expensive special equipment to make sure it was strong enough. Lampposts were deemed unsafe for hanging illuminations.

John Sunday earned the nickname of 'Grudge Sunday' as his unpopularity grew. The village shop was told it could no longer have wooden shelves which had been there since the time of Queen Victoria 'in case someone ran their hands along the shelves and got a splinter'. The village school was ordered to leave lights on at night 'in case unauthorized intruders tripped over in the dark'.

And children were warned not to play with 'counterfeit banknotes' after playing with toy money that did not show a picture of the Queen.

Grudge Sunday swelled in importance after each report. He thought the hatred directed towards him by the villagers of Carsely was prompted by envy.

All this Agatha learned when she called on her friend, Mrs Bloxby, the vicar's wife, a day after she had arrived home. But to Mrs Bloxby's surprise, Agatha did not seem particularly interested in the iniquities of Grudge Sunday. In fact Agatha did not seem to be interested in anything. When asked when she was going back to work, Agatha said listlessly, 'Probably some time in the New Year.'

Mrs Bloxby had often wished that her friend would grow out of her silly obsessions, but, she thought, Agatha without an obsession seemed gutted somehow.

Agatha Raisin still presented a smart appearance. She had thick glossy brown hair, good skin, excellent legs, but a rather thick waist and small brown bearlike eyes. She was wearing a tailored dark-blue cashmere trouser suit over a gold silk blouse. But her generous mouth was turned down at the corners and her eyes were dull.

'Our Ladies' Society is having a meeting with the Odley Cruesis society tonight. Do come along. They come under the rule of Mr Sunday and they wish us to join forces to see if there is something we can do. You haven't been to the society for ages.'

'I won't know anyone,' said Agatha. 'People keep selling up and the incomers get older and older.'

'Apart from myself and Miss Simms,' said Mrs Bloxby, 'you never cared much for the last lot. Oh, do come along.' Her usually mild and pleasant voice took on an edge. 'What else are you going to do? Sit at home and brood?'

Agatha gave her friend a startled look. In the tradition of the society they addressed each other by their second names, dating from some now long-forgotten time when the use of first names had been considered vulgar.

'I just can't seem to get interested in anything or anyone,' sighed Agatha. 'All right, I'll drive you over. I've never been to Odley Cruesis.'

'It's a pretty village. Nice people. The meeting is to be held in the vicarage. The vicar's wife, Penelope Timson, is an excellent baker. Her cakes are the talk of the neighbourhood.'

Odley Cruesis was situated ten miles from Carsely, reached along winding roads glittering with frost. With its old Tudor thatched houses, it seemed a little part of England that time had forgotten. To Agatha's dismay, cars were parked bumper to bumper outside the vicarage. 'I'll never be able to park,' she moaned.

'Yes, you will,' said Mrs Bloxby. 'There's a space right there.'

'I'm not driving a Mini,' said Agatha.

'Let me. I'll park it for you.'

Agatha got out and Mrs Bloxby got into the driver's seat and then parked Agatha's Rover neatly between two cars, leaving only inches on either side.

Agatha walked up to the vicarage. She could faintly hear the chatter of voices. She sighed. Cakes and boredom. Why had she come?

The vicarage drawing room was large. There seemed to be around twenty-five people there. But apart from Miss Simms, Agatha could not recognize anyone else from Carsely. Mrs Bloxby whispered in a disappointed voice that they must have decided not to attend. Agatha waved to Miss Simms, Carsely's unmarried mother, who was wearing a very short skirt, pixie boots, one of those fake French fisherman's jerseys, and long dangling earrings. There was a log fire on the hearth giving out a dim glow and occasionally sending puffs of smoke into the room.

Agatha refused tea and cakes. She could not be bothered to balance a teacup and plate. All the comfortable chairs had been taken up. Extra hard chairs had been brought in. Agatha sat down in a hard chair and wondered how long this wretched evening was going to last. The room was cold. Long French windows had been let into one wall of the old building and she could see steam from the breaths of all the cold visitors beginning to form on the glass.

A new arrival was being greeted with great enthusiasm. Agatha judged her to be in her seventies. She had leathery brown skin criss-crossed with wrinkles, thick black hair streaked with grey, and sparkling blue-grey eyes. 'Freezing out there,' she said, divesting herself of her coat and pashmina. 'They say we're going to have a blizzard tonight.'

'Who is she and what's that accent?' asked Agatha.

'She's Mrs Miriam Courtney, widow, South African, millionairess,' whispered Mrs Bloxby. 'She bought the manor house here about two years ago.'

Miriam looked brightly around the room. 'Am I expected to sit on one of those bum-numbing seats?'

'Have my chair,' said Miss Simms eagerly, surrendering her armchair.

Agatha felt a twinge of jealousy.

'Goodness, it's cold,' said Miriam. 'You've got coal in the scuttle over there. Why not throw some of that on the fire and get up a blaze?'

'It's not smokeless,' protested Penelope Timson, a tall thin woman with very large hands and feet and stooped shoulders, as if she had become bent after years of bending down to speak to smaller parishioners. She was wearing two cardigans over a sweater, a baggy tweed skirt, and woollen stockings which ended surprisingly in a pair of fluffy pink slippers in the shape of two large pink mice. 'You know what Mr Sunday is like. He tours around looking for smoke. We're supposed to burn smokeless.'

'Oh, never mind him. Courage. Chuck on a few lumps,' urged Miriam.

Bowing to a stronger will, Penelope picked up the tongs and deposited a few lumps. A blaze sprang up but the fire smoked even more.

'Damn, I brought brandy and I've left it in the car. I'll go and get it,' said Miriam. 'Don't wait for me. Get started.'

'I thought we weren't supposed to drink and drive,' muttered Agatha.

'She's probably thinking of herself,' said Mrs Bloxby. 'She can walk home. I wonder she bothered to drive.'

'I wonder anyone local bothered to drive,' said Agatha. 'Couldn't they just walk?'

'It's only in cities that people walk, I think,' said Mrs Bloxby. 'These days, in the country, people seem to drive even a few yards.'

Penelope called the meeting to order. Agatha's thoughts drifted off. Perhaps she could rescue the little that was left of her holiday and go somewhere warm. But she didn't like beach holidays any more and

Miriam's skin was surely an example of what happened to women who baked in the sun. It was all so stupid, reflected Agatha, this obsession with tanning. Understandable in the old days when only the rich went abroad in the winter and people wanted to appear jet-setters, but now the British from every walk of life flew out to exotic destinations, visiting a tanning parlour before they left. I mean, thought Agatha, you wouldn't leave a fine piece of leather out in the sun to dry and crack, so why do it with your skin? She remembered the slogan, 'Black is beautiful.' Quite right, too. But if she invented a slogan saying, 'White is beautiful,' she'd probably end up before the Race Relations Board.

Then she became aware that Penelope was asking, 'Where is Mrs Courtney? She should be back. I hope she hasn't slipped on ice.'

'I'll go and look for her,' said Miss Simms eagerly.

The meeting went on. Descriptions of the iniquities of Grudge Sunday wandered in and out of Agatha's brain. She wondered where her ex-husband was and reflected on how glad she was that she had got over her obsession for him, and yet, how empty life seemed without it.

'Found her! Mrs Courtney had to go home for the hooch. It wasn't in the car,' cried Miss Simms from the doorway. She came into the room followed by Miriam. Both were carrying bottles. Penelope went off to find glasses and returned with a tray full of them.

The room was soon full of genteel murmurs – 'Oh, I am sure one wouldn't hurt.' 'Such a cold night, one does need something.' 'Ooh, not so much!' – as brandy was poured.

'I think it's going to snow,' said Miriam. 'The wind's getting up.'

'Too cold for snow,' said Agatha, prompted by a sudden desire to contradict Miriam on any subject she cared to bring up.

The room was filling up with smoke. Penelope batted at it ineffectually with her large hands. 'Must get the sweep in,' she said.

She stared at the French windows and screamed. The tray she was holding, with a few remaining glasses, fell to the floor. Everyone stood up, turned and looked towards the French windows and soon the smoky air was full of cries.

His face pressed against the glass, his bloodied hands smearing the windowpanes as he slowly sank down, was John Sunday. Seen dimly through the steamy glass, it all looked unreal, like something out of a horror movie.

Agatha was never to forget that long night. They were trapped in the cold vicarage drawing room. The scene-of-crime operatives in their white suits worked outside the windows while a policeman stood guard. They seemed to take forever. Then there was a long wait for the arrival of the Home Office pathologist. After he was finished, Detective Inspector Wilkes, with Agatha's friend Detective Sergeant Bill Wong and one of Agatha's pet hates Detective Sergeant Collins, an acidulous woman, arrived. One by one they were interviewed. Bill went on as if he did not know Agatha, apart

14

from muttering to her that he would call on her some-time. Collins insisted they were all breathalyzed before they were pronounced fit to drive home. Miriam and Miss Simms were taken off for questioning, being the only two to have left the room.

To add to all the misery, when Agatha and Mrs Bloxby left the vicarage, it had warmed up just enough for snow and it was coming down heavily. The cars which had been parked in front and behind Agatha's had already driven off.

Snow danced hypnotically in front of her and whitened the road in front as she drove along the narrow lanes.

Agatha dropped Mrs Bloxby at the vicarage in Carsely and then drove home, edging her way through the white wilderness.

Her sleepy cats came to meet her. Agatha glanced at her watch. Five in the morning! She was bone tired but the palms of her hands were tingling. A murder!

Her last waking thought was that she must get back to the office.

She awoke late the next day to find snow piled against the windows. The central heating did not seem to be coping very well. Huddled in a dressing gown, Agatha went down to her living room and lit the fire that her cleaner, Doris Simpson, had laid ready in the grate. Then she went through to the kitchen to prepare her breakfast – one cup of black coffee. She retreated to the living room and phoned Toni Gilmour, knowing that her young assistant lived around the corner from the office and would be on duty.

'How was your holiday?' asked Toni.

'Foul. I'll tell you about it later. There's been a murder.'

Agatha outlined what had happened, ending with, 'John Sunday appears to have made so many enemies around the villages that it's going to be hard to find the culprit. Maybe he made some enemies at work. Could you check with the Mircester Health and Safety Board? And ask Patrick to find out from his old police contacts if there's any news of exactly how he died.'

Patrick Mulligan, a retired policeman, had worked for Agatha for some time, along with Phil Marshall, an elderly man from Carsely, Sharon Gold, a bouncy young friend of Toni's, and Mrs Freedman, the agency's secretary. Paul Kenson and Fred Auster, who had briefly worked for her, had left to work for a security firm in Iraq.

Agatha fretted as she glared out at the still-falling snow. She made herself a cheese sandwich and another cup of coffee and switched on the television to BBC news. There was a global warming demonstration in Trafalgar Square with protestors nearly obliterated on the screen by the driving snow. She sat patiently through the whole of the news but there was nothing on the murder of John Sunday.

The day dragged on in its dreary whiteness. Agatha's two cats, Hodge and Boswell, sat patiently by the kitchen door, wondering why Agatha did not let them out.

The phone rang at midday. It was Toni. She said that

Patrick had little news other than that the police had said it looked as if Sunday had been stabbed with something like a kitchen knife. He had tried to defend himself and there were cuts on his hands and forearms.

Agatha relapsed into a snowbound torpor. She fell asleep on the sofa in the afternoon, only awakening an hour later at the ringing of her doorbell.

On opening the door, she found Miriam Courtney on her doorstep, unbuckling a pair of skis. 'The snow's stopped and I thought I'd come and see you,' said Miriam. 'The gritters haven't been out on the village roads but the farmers had snowploughed them so I put on my skis and came over. Thank goodness the snow has stopped. Aren't you going to ask me in?'

'Sorry,' said Agatha. 'Come in.'

Miriam propped her skis against the outside wall. 'Come through to the kitchen,' said Agatha. She had taken a dislike to Miriam but decided that any company was preferable to none. 'Coffee?'

'Sure.' Miriam took off her padded coat and woolly hat and sat down at the kitchen table.

'What brings you?' asked Agatha, plugging in the electric coffee percolator.

'I heard you have a detective agency and I want to hire you. I'm prime suspect.'

'Why?'

'Because I was the one person, apart from Miss Simms, who was out of the room for any length of time. Furthermore, I am on record as having called at the offices of the Health and Safety Board in Mircester and threatened to kill Sunday.'

17

'Why?'

'Because in the summer I open the manor to the public twice a week. It's an old Tudor building. I get a good number of tours. Sunday said the steps up to the front door made it impossible for the disabled to have access. I would have to have a ramp. The ramp they suggested was a great metal thing that seemed to stretch halfway down the drive. I said in the past that the rare visitor in a wheelchair was just wheeled backwards up the very shallow steps. Sunday said that unless I had the ramp, I could no longer open the house to the public. I said I'd kill the stupid bureaucratic bastard. The police turned up this morning at the manor with a search warrant.'

'How did they get through the snow?' asked Agatha, putting down a cup of coffee in front of Miriam.

'They got through somehow in Land Rovers. Took all my kitchen knives away. I want you to find out who really did it. I'm an outsider in that village. The trouble's started already. The two women who clean for me phoned up this morning to say they would no longer work for me.'

'Why do you need to open the manor to the public? Do you need the money?'

'Not a bit of it. But I enjoy showing the place off. I've done an awful lot of restoration.'

'I haven't a contract here but I'll get the office to send you one to sign,' said Agatha. 'Can you think of anyone?'

'He offended so many people, I can't suggest where you should start. Listen! That's the gritter at last.'

18

'Good,' said Agatha. 'I've been getting cabin fever sitting here.'

'Isn't that someone at your door?'

Agatha went to answer. The muffled figure of Sir Charles Fraith, one of Agatha's closest friends, stood there. 'Gosh, I thought I'd never get here,' he said, stamping snow from his boots. 'I had to borrow the gardener's Land Rover. My drive is like the Cresta Run. I heard about the murder on the morning news.'

Charles followed Agatha into the kitchen and she introduced him to Miriam. 'A "sir",' said Miriam. 'How grand!' To Agatha's irritation, she was almost coquettish.

Miriam went on to explain the reason for her visit. 'Oh, Aggie will sort you out,' said Charles, helping himself to coffee.

Charles was a medium-sized man with immaculately barbered hair and neat features. Agatha often thought he was as self-contained as her cats. He came and went in and out of her life, often using her cottage as a sort of hotel.

'You didn't use your keys,' said Agatha. 'Have you lost the keys to my cottage?'

'No, but you got shirty the last time I just walked in.'

Miriam looked from one to the other, her eyes sparkling with interest. 'Are you two an item?'

'No!' said Agatha. 'But no time like the present. I'd like to get back to Odley Cruesis and see what I can dig up.'

'I'll drive you over,' said Charles. 'How did you get here, Miriam?'

'On my skis.'

Charles laughed. 'What a lady. I've got a roof rack for your skis. We can all go together.'

Agatha turned away quickly to hide the scowl on her face. She had few friends and was jealous and possessive of the ones she had. 'I'll just go upstairs and change.'

As Agatha put on warm clothes, she could hear Miriam's peals of laughter followed by appreciative chuckles from Charles.

I bet the fact she's employing me is a blind, thought Agatha. I bet she did it. Please God, let Miriam be the murderer.

Chapter Two

'This is my showpiece,' said Miriam proudly, leading them into the main hall of the manor.

Charles looked around at the gleaming suits of armour, the long refectory table, the crossed halberds on the wall, the tattered battle flags, and the imitation gas-fired flambeaux and suppressed a smile. He doubted if there was one authentic piece in the room. But Agatha was obviously jealous of Miriam and he felt like winding her up further. Maybe Agatha might begin to recognize some of her worst qualities, such as pushiness, in Miriam and tone down a bit.

'Lovely!' he exclaimed.

Agatha felt it all looked like a stage set. 'Now, can I get you something to drink?' asked Miriam. 'I feel we are all going to be great friends.' But she turned her back on Agatha as she said this and smiled broadly at Charles.

'I think it would be a good idea if we got started,' said Agatha loudly. 'Let's begin at the vicarage.'

A mobile police unit had been set up in the little triangle

of village green in the centre of Odley Cruesis. Police tape fenced off the front of the vicarage. A policeman stood on guard outside the door.

Agatha ducked under the tape, followed by Miriam and Charles. 'You can't come in here,' protested the policeman.

'The murder took place outside,' said Agatha, pointing to the tented-off French windows. 'We are making a social call.'

The policeman looked across at the mobile police unit as if for help and then to the tent where shadowy figures moved under halogen lights. 'Wait here,' he ordered and strode off towards the police unit.

As they shivered in the snow and waited, Agatha asked Miriam, 'What brought you to the Cotswolds?'

'I came here on a holiday years ago and never forgot it. So beautiful and peaceful. Well, up till now, that is. Oh, here's the copper.'

'You can go in,' said the policeman. 'Mrs Courtney?'

'Yes, that's me.'

'You're to come with me to the police unit for more questioning.'

'Really!' complained Miriam, exasperated. 'You've already kept me up most of the night. You'll be hearing from my lawyer as soon as he can get through the snow.'

She walked off with the policeman and Agatha went up to the door of the vicarage and rang the bell.

Penelope answered the door. She was wearing the same outfit as she had done the night before. Agatha wondered if she had slept in her clothes. Penelope blinked at them myopically. 'If you are the press,' she said, 'I have nothing to say.'

'I'm Agatha Raisin,' said Agatha, 'and this is my friend, Sir Charles Fraith.'

Penelope beamed. 'I am so sorry I didn't recognize you, Sir Charles. I attended a fête in the grounds of your beautiful house last year. Do come in.' She seemed to have forgotten Agatha's existence.

The drawing room of the old vicarage was colder than ever. A two-bar electric heater had been placed in front of the ash-filled hearth. A tall thin man came into the room. 'This is my husband,' said Penelope, making introductions all round. He shook hands with them.

'I'm Giles Timson,' he said in a high, reedy voice. 'Bad business, heh? Do sit down.'

'I am a friend of Mrs Bloxby,' began Agatha, settling herself in an armchair beside the heater. 'I run a detective agency. Mrs Courtney has hired me to investigate.'

'Why?' he asked. He looked like a surprised heron looking down at an odd fish in a pool as he stood over Agatha. He had grey hair and a long thin nose.

'Miriam seems to be considered number one suspect.'

'I'm sure the police will find the culprit,' he said.

'So distressing,' fluted Penelope. 'I mean, it's not a case of who would have wanted to murder John Sunday, but who wouldn't?'

'My dear . . .'

'Well, Giles, you yourself said you would like to murder the little man.'

'What prompted that?' asked Charles.

'I don't think . . .' began the vicar nervously, but

Penelope said eagerly, 'Oh, you remember, he objected to candles in the church. He said they might fall over and burn someone. You were so angry, Giles. "I could kill you, you little insect," that's what you said. Giles has quite a temper.'

'I am glad they don't have hanging any more,' said the vicar, 'or my dear wife would have me on the scaffold. I'll be in my study if anyone wants me.' His pale grey eyes raked up and down his wife's thin figure. 'Didn't you change your clothes this morning?'

'There wasn't time. The police were here all night and I slept in the armchair by the fire.'

'Tcha!' said the vicar and left the room.

'Was there anyone here last night who might have a reason to kill Sunday?' asked Agatha.

'Oh, dear. I mean, I don't think anyone would have *murdered* him, but the reason for the meeting was that everyone had run foul of the dreadful man at one time or another.'

'What sort of things?'

'Mrs Carrie Brother was charged by him because her dog fouled the village green. Mr and Mrs Summer and Mr and Mrs Beagle – they usually decorate their cottages with Christmas lights but have been stopped this year. All those regulations.'

'Where were they seated?' asked Agatha.

'It's so hard to remember. I think the Beagles were by the fire and the Summers over by the door. But it would need to be someone who left the room, wouldn't it? There's only Mrs Courtney and Miss Simms. Perhaps Miss Simms?'

24

'Did she voice a dislike of Sunday?'

'Well, no, but I mean, she is not really quite what one would expect at a ladies society.'

Agatha bristled. 'Miss Simms has been a very good secretary for some time.'

'I don't think it can be Miriam,' said Charles with a sideways glinting smile at Agatha. 'She seems such a jolly, straightforward sort of person.'

'Exactly,' said Penelope. 'And she has done so much for the village. Such a generous contribution to the church restoration fund and she always makes the manor available for village parties and events.'

Again that stab of jealousy hit Agatha. Would anyone praise her in such a way? Sometimes she felt she was living *on* the Cotswolds rather than *in* the Cotswolds. Her work at the agency meant she was often out of the village for long periods of time. In the past she had fund-raised for various charities but certainly not of late. And the recession meant that people were always arriving to take up the houses the new impoverished were leaving, so few people would remember her actually doing anything to help the village of Carsely. Agatha wished she had paid more attention to the people in the room the previous night.

'Did John Sunday have a love life?' asked Charles.

Penelope removed one pink slipper and meditatively scratched a big toe. 'Chilblains,' she said. 'There was a rumour . . . oh, but I never pay attention to gossip.'

'Try to remember,' said Agatha eagerly.

'I shouldn't . . . and Giles would be furious if he knew

25

I had been passing on malicious gossip, but I did hear that Tilly Glossop and he seemed to be close.'

'And where does this Tilly Glossop live?'

'On the other side of the green. It's a little cottage called Happenstance.'

'That's an odd name,' said Charles.

'She is rather an odd woman. Quite gypsy-like. I don't think she has any gypsy blood in her but she wears bangles and shawls and thingies.'

Agatha got to her feet. 'No time like the present. We'll go and talk to her.'

'Dear me,' fluttered Penelope. 'You won't say I—'

'No, no. Won't breathe a word. Was she here last night?'

'No, she wasn't. She doesn't go to church either.'

'Does anyone these days?' asked Agatha cynically.

'My dear Mrs Raisin. Most of this village attends on Sundays.'

As Agatha and Charles, hanging on to each other, staggered through the snow to the other side of the green, Charles said, 'You're slipping, Agatha.'

'I know I am. These boots were not made for walking.'

'I don't mean that. There was another person out of that room last night surely?'

'Who?'

'Was the vicar there?'

'Well, no.'

'And he's got a bad temper *and* he threatened to kill the little twat.'

'I thought of him,' lied Agatha huffily, 'but I thought I would explore that avenue later.'

'Says you!'

'Says I. Here we are,' said Agatha.

Happenstance was a very old cottage, which leaned towards the garden under a heavy snow-covered thatched roof. Two front windows looked like eyes.

'The air's suddenly turned warmer,' said Charles. 'Everything's beginning to drip. And the sun's coming out.'

Agatha rang the bell. No one answered. 'Maybe the bell doesn't work,' said Charles. 'Give the door a good bang.'

Agatha hammered on the door. But her banging precipitated a small avalanche of snow from the roof which cascaded down on them.

'Snakes and bastards,' howled Agatha.

'Let's give up,' said Charles. 'Damn, I've got snow down the back of my neck.'

'What do you want?' demanded a voice behind them.

They both swung round. The round figure of a woman muffled up in a coat and two shawls with a woolly cap pulled down over her face stood glaring at them.

'We just wanted a word with you,' said Agatha. 'I am a private detective working for Miriam Courtney. This is Sir Charles Fraith.'

'Oh, if you're working for Miriam, you'd best come indoors. But leave your coats in the hall. You're covered with snow.'

She pushed past them and opened the door. The 'hall'

was a tiny space cluttered up with Wellington boots and coats on pegs on the wall. Agatha looked for a spare peg but could find none. She took off her coat and rammed it over a hanging oilskin. Charles dropped his on the floor.

Tilly Glossop had disappeared somewhere. They stood irresolute until they heard her call, 'In here.'

The sound of her voice came from the left. They pushed open the door and entered a cluttered cottage parlour. A fire smouldered in the grate. The mantelpiece above it was crowded with china ornaments. One wall was covered with bookshelves full of paperbacks. A computer and printer were set up on a table at the window. The three-piece suite so beloved by English households was missing. Instead three hard-backed chairs fronted a low coffee table.

Divested of her outer garments – where had she put them? wondered Agatha – she was revealed as a stocky middle-aged woman with a swarthy face and large black eyes. She had a small curved nose like a beak and a thin mouth. She was dressed in a lumpy wool cardigan and black T-shirt over a baggy skirt.

'So what do you want to know?' asked Tilly. 'Sit down.'

Agatha and Charles sat down on two of the hard chairs and Tilly stood in front of them with her back to the fire.

'We heard you were a friend of John Sunday,' said Agatha, miserably aware that her boots were now full of melting snow.

'I knew him. So what?'

'Did he have any enemies?'

'Of course he had, you stupid woman. Anyone trying to bring a little law and order always has enemies.'

'Anyone more threatening than the others?'

'Well, there was Carrie.'

'Carrie Brother?' asked Agatha. 'The one whose dog fouled the village green?'

'That's the one. Great hulking brute of a woman. Swore at poor John like a trooper.'

'Were you having an affair with John Sunday?'

'We were friends, that's all.'

'May I ask what you had in common?'

'I'll tell you what we had in common,' snarled Tilly. 'A hatred of all the mealy-mouthed parochial little insects called villagers.'

Charles found his voice. He asked mildly, 'If you dislike the people in the village so much, why do you live here?'

'They're the incomers, not me. This was my parents' cottage and my grandparents' before them. They come and they go, trying to fit into village life, or some Merchant Ivory view of village life. House prices rise so they sell up and off they go back to their cities. I liked seeing John making them sweat.'

'Did you see him on the evening of the murder?' asked Agatha.

Something flickered in those obsidian eyes of hers but she said curtly, 'No.'

'Are you interested in finding out who murdered him?' asked Charles.

She shrugged her meaty shoulders. 'I would be if I thought the police would ever find the culprit, but they won't.'

'Why?' asked Agatha.

She grinned, revealing very white dentures. 'Too many suspects. Now, why don't you push off?'

'I don't like her and I'm freezing,' moaned Agatha when they drove off. 'Let's get home and change. Then we'll go back and tackle Carrie Brother.'

'We, paleface?'

'You mean you're leaving?'

'People to see, places to go,' said Charles.

Agatha would have liked to protest but realized she had no claim on him. He didn't work for her.

Outside her cottage, Charles got into his own car and sped off. Agatha felt rather bereft. He had not said if he would be back.

Inside, Agatha's cleaner, Doris Simpson, was hard at work. She switched off the vacuum when she saw Agatha and said, 'Terrible, that murder. Not that he didn't deserve it, though.'

'I must get changed,' said Agatha, heading for the stairs.

'I'll make you a nice strong cup of coffee,' Doris called after her.

Agatha had a hot shower and put on dry clothes. Back in the kitchen, Doris put a mug of coffee down on the kitchen table. 'Have you heard of anyone who might have wanted to kill Sunday?' asked Agatha.

'Lots of people,' said Doris. 'But not the kind that'd actually do it. Like our vicar. They're putting the tree up on the church and the lights up in the village street.'

'Won't they get into trouble?'

'No, John was disliked at the Health and Safety. Insisted on shoving everything through and making work for his colleagues they didn't want.'

'There's an idea,' said Agatha slowly. 'Of course. I was thinking they were all bastards on that Safety Board. Maybe he really wound someone up. But who would follow him in a blizzard to a small village?'

'Drink your coffee, love. I'll just get on.' Doris left the kitchen. Agatha's cats, who adored the cleaner, scampered after her. Agatha watched them sourly. Charles, who was like a cat, had been smarming all over Miriam, and her treacherous cats seemed to always prefer Doris to herself.

She felt lonely. She suddenly did not want to go back to Odley Cruesis and detect on her own.

Agatha phoned Toni. Mrs Freedman said Toni was out of the office. Agatha told her to draw up a contract for Miriam Courtney, gave her the address and told her to express post it. Then Agatha called Toni on her mobile. 'I'm heading in your direction,' said Toni cheerfully. 'It's quiet here today. I think everyone's saving their money for Christmas and the recession has been hitting us a bit. Be with you in about ten minutes.'

Agatha brightened up. Although she was occasionally jealous of young Toni's good looks and successful detecting, she was fond of the girl.

Toni duly arrived, her face glowing with health. She was a slim girl in her late teens with natural blonde hair, good skin and a perfect figure. 'It's getting slushy really fast,' said Toni cheerfully. 'Phil has gone round to Sunday's office to see if he can find out if anyone there hated him enough to kill him. So what exactly happened?'

Agatha told her about the protest meeting and about the horror of seeing the dying Sunday at the window. 'Only Miss Simms and Miriam Courtney left the room. I was so bored my mind kept drifting. I wasn't paying much attention. Do you want a coffee or something or shall we go?'

'Let's go,' said Toni. 'I'll have a coffee later. Does the village have a pub?'

'I didn't notice one. Why?'

'Could be a good source of gossip.'

Odley Cruesis glittered under a yellow sun. The air was full of the sound of running water. Agatha parked by the village green. Wearing Wellington boots this time, she stumbled through the slush and stopped a villager to ask directions to the pub.

'Can't rightly be doing that, m'dear,' said a gnarled old man.

'And why is that?'

'Pub closed down last year.'

'There you are!' exclaimed Agatha, as she and Toni looked around. 'Another centre of village life gone and all because of that ridiculous smoking ban.'

'But the papers say it's because of all the cheap booze in supermarkets,' protested Toni.

'The newspapers are so politically correct, they make me sick,' said Agatha. 'The minute the smoking ban came in, pubs started closing down all over the place. Move on. There's that horrible Collins woman glaring at us.'

The detective was standing on the steps of the mobile police unit, staring at them.

'Move on where?' asked Toni.

'There's the village shop. I want to speak to someone called Carrie Brother.'

The little shop was a dark, depressing place. The woman behind the counter told Agatha that Mrs Brother lived at number nine, a cottage just to their left. 'Her don't hold with giving names to liddle cottages,' said the woman.

Number nine was a two-storied Queen Anne building with a lintel over the door. Agatha rang the bell and cringed at the sound of a volley of barking. 'I thought the wretched woman had only one dog,' muttered Agatha. The barking stopped abruptly as a heavyset woman answered the door, clutching a small Yorkshire terrier.

'You're that detective who's investigating for Miriam,' said Carrie. 'Come in.'

'How did you hear?' asked Agatha as Carrie ushered them into a pleasant room on the ground floor.

'News travels fast here. Now, what can I do for you?'
'It's about John Sunday.'
Carrie grinned.
'It's a fair cop. I did it.'

Chapter Three

Agatha eyed her warily. Carrie was a big strong woman, possibly in her late forties. Everything about her was big, from her large head, topped with a thick mane of brown curly hair, to her large hands and feet.

'I've left something in the car,' said Toni and ran out of the house.

Good, thought Agatha, she's gone for the police.

'How did you do it?' asked Agatha in what she hoped was a gentle, coaxing voice.

'Sit down!' said Carrie.

'Where are the other dogs?' asked Agatha nervously.

'Here,' said Carrie. She pressed a button on a machine on a small table next to her and the air was suddenly full of barking. She switched it off.

'Great stuff. Good burglar repellent. You want to know how I did it? Telekinesis.'

Agatha blinked. 'Tele-what?'

'I have a powerful mind. I hated that little toad. I saw him skulking around the village last night. I put my hands to my forehead, so. I transferred my thoughts to the big kitchen knife in the kitchen and caused it to rise up. I opened the front door and sent it towards the vicarage . . .'

The door crashed open and Toni, followed by Bill Wong, Collins and two policemen, rushed into the room.

'Leave this to us,' said Collins, glaring at Agatha.

'I'm staying right here,' said Agatha mutinously. 'What were you saying, Mrs Brother?'

'Miss, please.' Carrie began her tale of telekinesis again. When she had finished, she burst out laughing. 'You should just see your faces,' she chortled. 'Gotcha!'

Collins said in a thin voice to one of the policemen, 'Take Mizz Brother over to the police unit and charge her with wasting police time.'

'Here, wait a bit. Can't you take a joke?' protested Carrie as she was led off, still clutching her Yorkshire terrier to her massive bosom.

Collins then rounded on Agatha. 'Just mind your own business in future or I'll book you as well,' she said. 'Come along, Wong.'

Agatha and Toni followed them out. Collins had just reached the doorstep, slippery with slush, when Agatha switched on the dog-barking recorder. Collins jumped nervously and slipped and sat down in a puddle of slush on the doorstep. Agatha switched off the machine and stepped neatly round Collins, followed by Toni.

'I really don't know where that noise came from,' she said sweetly. 'Bye.'

They hurried off to the car. 'I wish I could have a word with Bill in private,' said Agatha.

'What now?' asked Toni.

'We'll drive along to the manor and see Miriam. How's your friend Sharon been getting on?'

'All right,' said Toni.

Agatha turned the car into the drive of the manor house. She switched off the engine and slewed round to look at Toni. 'When I asked you about Sharon, that "all right" sounded a bit muted. What's going on?'

Toni sighed. 'It's just that she's quarrelled with her parents and moved in with me. I've only got that small flat, as you know, and, well, it's all a bit claustrophobic. She's messy and I like things neat. She dyes her hair a lot, different colours, and there are streaks of dye on the hand basin and in the bath. I've started snapping and complaining a lot. I don't want to lose her friendship, but things are very strained.'

'I pay her a good salary. She could afford a place of her own.'

'I didn't like to suggest it. She'll think I'm throwing her out.'

'I'll speak to her.'

'Don't do that! She'll be hurt if she thinks I've been complaining about her.'

'I'm the soul of tact,' said Agatha. 'I'll call on the pair of you this evening.'

Toni groaned inwardly. Agatha's idea of tact was anyone else's idea of direct rudeness.

The door of the manor opened and Miriam stood on the step. 'Are you coming in?' she called.

'Bet she did it,' muttered Agatha as they got out of the car.

*　*　*

Toni looked around the main hall in awe. 'This is magnificent,' she said.

Miriam beamed. 'What a nice girl you are. I do like your daughter, Agatha.'

'Toni is not my daughter. She is a detective who works for me.'

'She's very young,' commented Miriam with a sly smile, 'but *very* attractive.'

Is she hinting I'm a lesbian? thought Agatha furiously.

Aloud, she said, 'Is there somewhere less draughty and cold where we can talk?'

'Follow me,' said Miriam.

She led the way through a small door at the end of the hall and into a wood-panelled room with comfortable chairs, where a fire burned brightly on the hearth. 'I can't have central heating,' said Miriam, 'in case it warps the antiques.'

The only genuine antique here is you, thought Agatha. This manor is jammed with fakes.

They all sat down in front of the fire. 'Want a drink?' asked Miriam.

'Coffee would be nice,' said Agatha.

Miriam stood up and pulled on an embroidered bell rope by the fireplace. 'Isn't this fun?' she said. 'The old bell rope was frayed and a little woman in the village made up a new one.'

'Do you have a large staff?' asked Agatha.

'No. Some of the village women come in to clean but I keep a Ukrainian girl to act as a sort of maid.'

The door opened and a small, neat girl came in dressed in black with a white apron and cap.

'Coffee, Natasha,' ordered Miriam.

'Doesn't she object to looking like a Victorian servant?' asked Agatha when the maid had left.

'How should I know?' said Miriam rudely. 'I didn't ask her. It impresses the tourists. I advertise in America and often get coach tours descending on me. Now, let's get down to business. I don't like being suspected of this murder.'

'There seem to be so many people who might have wanted John Sunday dead,' said Agatha. 'All we can do is ferret around.'

'I can do that as well,' said Miriam brightly. 'I know everyone in this village.'

'So far,' said Agatha, 'all we have learned is that Tilly Glossop was close to Sunday and may have been having an affair with him. Carrie Brother confessed to doing the murder by telekinesis as a joke and is being charged by the police for wasting their time. The vicar threatened to kill Sunday for banning candles in the church. Anyone else?'

'There are the Summers and the Beagles,' said Miriam. 'They decorated their cottages each year with masses of Christmas lights and illuminated plastic Santas in the gardens. Yuck! We were all rather pleased when Sunday put a stop to that. Let down the tone of the place no end.'

'What reasons did he give?'

'Oh, you know . . . Thank you, Natasha, leave the tray on the table and we will help ourselves. Light bulbs had to be subjected to a "pull" test, their carbon footprint was the size of a hobnailed boot, dangerous electrical wiring, you name it.'

'Can you see any of them murdering someone?' asked Toni.

'Go and see them. They're all old and frail.'

'If they are that old and frail,' said Agatha, 'how did they get all the decorations up?'

'Old Fred Summer did most of the work. He's a retired builder. Charlie Beagle is a retired electrician. Both of them competed a bit to see who could get the most lights up but it was a friendly competition.'

'Where do they live?' asked Agatha.

'The last two cottages out on the Badsey road.'

Miriam poured coffee. Agatha noticed the coffee was served in earthenware mugs. She began to wonder if Miriam was as wealthy as she was reputed to be or someone who had turned an old manor house into a Disneyfied attraction for tourists.

'You seem to have a very good track record as a detective,' said Miriam. 'One wouldn't think it to look at you. Charles told me you were a wiz at ferreting things out.'

'I have had a lot of success,' said Agatha, repressing a sudden impulse to throw her coffee cup at Miriam's head.

'I bet I'd make a pretty good detective. I'll ask Charles when I see him.'

'I doubt if you will,' said Agatha.

'Oh, he's taking me for dinner tonight. We arranged it earlier.'

He's *my* friend, not *yours*, thought Agatha savagely. She wished she'd never taken Miriam on as a client. She felt that this woman was going to move into her life and circle of friends and take over.

Aloud she said, 'Can you think of anyone else in this village before I get back to Mircester? I really must call in at the office.'

'Let me think.' Miriam scowled down into her coffee cup. Then her face cleared. 'Of course. I'd forgotten. May Dinwoody. She makes toys and sells them at the markets. Sunday damned them as unsafe for children and quite ruined her business. God, was she ever furious.'

'Where will I find her?'

'In the old mill house at the back of the shop, down that lane that runs at the side.'

'We'll try her. Come along, Toni.' Agatha rose to her feet.

'I'll call on you later,' said Miriam.

'Don't bother. I've got other work to do,' said Agatha, heading for the door. 'I'll keep you posted.'

'Snakes and bastards,' muttered Agatha as they got back into her car. 'I really don't like her.'

'We can't like all our clients,' commented Toni reasonably. 'We've had some horrors.'

'Look at how fast the snow is melting,' said Agatha. 'That's all the hopes of a white Christmas gone.' Night had fallen and a large moon was shining down.

'Are you having a party this Christmas?' asked Toni.

'Never again. What are you doing for Christmas?'

'Going to my mother's in Southampton.'

'Right. Here we are at the shop. Let's park here and walk.'

The old mill house had been divided into flats. It loomed over a weedy pond.

Agatha studied the names beside the front door and pressed a bell marked 'Flat 3, Dinwoody'. A tinny voice came over the intercom. Agatha explained who she was. There was a long silence and then the front door buzzed.

They entered and walked up carpeted stairs to the flat, which was on the first floor. A woman was waiting by the open door. Agatha's heart sank. May Dinwoody certainly did not look the type of lady to plunge a knife into anyone. She was possibly in her sixties, slightly stooped with grey hair and thick glasses, through which pale grey eyes stared at them myopically. She was wearing a pink T-shirt emblazoned in sequins with the slogan Born To Party, over which she wore a man's brown cardigan. She was also wearing black leggings and pixie boots. Agatha wondered whether she was a thrift shop junkie wearing a younger relative's clothes.

'Come in,' said May. 'I hear you are investigating this murder for Miriam.'

She stood back to let them past and then led them into a dimly lit room, filled with flowers and pictures. A square window looked over the pond. Moonlight sparkling on the water threw flickers of wavering light into the room.

'Take your coats off,' urged May. Her voice held a

Scottish burr. 'The central heating here is excellent. Now, coffee?'

'I think we've had enough coffee for one day,' said Agatha. She saw a large glass ashtray on a coffee table. 'Mind if I smoke?'

'Go ahead,' said May. 'I smoke myself. We are a persecuted race. First the smoking ban closed down the village pub and now they don't allow smoking on aircraft, the air is no longer changed and we all have to get slowly poisoned with gunk leaking from the engines. Pilots are trying to sue for brain damage but it keeps getting hushed up. I hate this politically correct nanny state.'

Agatha sat down in an armchair and lit a cigarette after offering one to May.

Soon smoke lay in bands across the room. Toni took a chair by the window, longing to open it, because the room was hot and stuffy and she did not want to suffer from passive smoking.

'Now,' said Agatha, 'I hear you had a row with Sunday.'

'I did so. Horrible wee man. Ruining my business, claiming my toys were unsafe. But I won! I took him to court and proved all my toys were well made and there was no danger of children choking on bits of them. The Health and Safety Board had to pay me compensation.'

'There's a thing,' said Agatha. 'Why on earth did they keep him on after that?'

'I can't imagine.'

'I can't remember seeing you at the protest meeting.'

'Having got satisfaction, I couldn't be bothered going. Penelope organized it and ineffectual is her middle name. I knew they'd all sit and talk and nothing would come out of it.'

'Can you think of anyone in this village who could get so riled up they might murder him?'

'To be honest, no. I think you should check out Mircester. Big towns are more likely places to find murderers than in this wee village.'

'It's late,' mourned Agatha as she drove off. 'I'll drop you at my place and you can pick up your car. I'm starving. Would you like something to eat?'

'Don't bother,' said Toni, who had experienced Agatha's cooking in the past.

'Right. I'll call on you later and see what we can do about Sharon.'

'I can cope myself.'

'No, you can't. I'll see you later.'

Charles had invited Miriam to dinner, partly to play detective and partly to annoy Agatha. The restaurant was a French one in the centre of Mircester.

To his surprise, Miriam had not dressed up in any way. She was wearing a much-washed sweater and droopy skirt. 'Don't let's speak yet,' said Miriam, gazing at Charles over the menu. 'I love my food and want to concentrate on ordering.'

Charles, who had hoped to get away with one dish each and coffee, decided to say – as he had done so many times with Agatha – that he had forgotten his wallet. He became even more determined on this course of action when he heard Miriam ordering a dozen large snails to begin, followed by turbot and asparagus. The turbot was criminally expensive.

Charles ordered a modest salad followed by a pepper steak. Miriam insisted on choosing the wine – 'I'm by way of being an expert.'

She scanned the wine list and then said brightly, 'I know, let's celebrate the beginning of our friendship, Charles.' She ordered a bottle of vintage champagne.

'When did your husband die?' asked Charles.

'He didn't. He's still alive. Widow sounds much more respectable. I caught him in bed with the help. Never had much luck. The one before him was a rat as well *and* the one before that.'

'How many times have you been married?'

'Just the three times. What about you?'

'Once. Didn't work out.'

'What about Agatha?'

'Two times.'

'Tell me about her.'

'If you want to know anything about Agatha Raisin, ask her yourself. I don't discuss my friends.'

Miriam's snails arrived. They were very large snails. She winkled each one out of its shell, popped it in her mouth and chewed, making *mmm mmm* sounds.

'What about this murder?' asked Charles. 'Did you do it?'

45

'My dear man! No, but I've been thinking hard and I've a pretty good idea who did it.'

'Who?'

She waved her two-pronged snail fork at him roguishly and a tiny drop of garlic butter flew across the table and landed on Charles' silk tie. 'Wouldn't you just like to know? But I'll tell you this. Tomorrow I'm cancelling the services of Agatha Raisin and going to the police. When I was getting the brandy, I saw something. Didn't think much of it at the time. It seemed so impossible. I—'

But Miriam had made the mistake of talking while she was eating and a snail lodged in her throat.

Charles stared as she made frantic noises. An efficient waiter rushed up, dragged Miriam to her feet and performed the Heimlich manoeuvre. The snail shot out and landed in Charles' lap.

Miriam thanked the waiter profusely, took a gulp of champagne and said, 'Sorry, Charles. I think I'd better go home. Remember to give that waiter a good tip.'

Charles tried to protest but Miriam exited the dining room at a remarkable speed.

He wondered whether they had a doggy bag for turbot.

Agatha entered Toni's little flat and looked narrowly at Sharon, who was sprawled on the sofa. Sharon was a bright, bouncy girl with large breasts, always displayed, no matter what the weather, in low-cut tops. Her hair changed colour weekly. That evening, it was flaming red. An empty pizza box was on the table in front of her along with two crushed beer cans.

'I thought I'd make a brief call on you to discuss the case,' said Agatha. 'Don't bother leaving, Sharon. As my employee, this concerns you as well.'

'Don't need to leave,' said Sharon. 'I live here now.'

'But Toni hasn't got room for you!'

'Oh, Tone doesn't mind. Me and Tone are friends.'

'But why did you move out of your family home?'

'Big stinking row with me dad.'

'Why?'

'Caught me smoking a spliff.'

'Sharon! The junk on the streets is dangerous.' Agatha's bearlike eyes bored into her. 'Do you like your job, Sharon?'

'Sure.'

'No drugs and pack up your stuff and get back home. Look at this place! It's a tip. Toni hasn't said anything but I can see you are causing her stress.'

'Don't want to go home,' wailed Sharon.

'I pay you enough to rent a flat,' said Agatha. 'Come along. Out of here tonight or out of a job tomorrow.'

'Toni!' begged Sharon.

'Don't say a word,' said Agatha. 'Get your things – now!'

Agatha felt weary by the time she had dealt with Sharon's parents. She did not want to fire Sharon as the girl had a natural bent when it came to detecting. She was just getting back into her car when her phone rang.

It was Charles. Agatha listened in amusement to his description of the aborted dinner, but her amusement died when he told her that Miriam was sure she knew the identity of the murderer.

'I'll get over there in the morning and choke it out of her,' said Agatha.

Miriam was lying in bed reading a literary novel. She was not enjoying it at all, but it had been nominated for the Booker Prize and Miriam only read to impress people with her knowledge of the latest literary talent. She had phoned Penelope Timson before she had gone to bed and had told her she was sure she knew the identity of the murderer. Penelope had asked for a name but Miriam had told her to wait and see. Now, she felt a bit silly and was sure she had imagined the whole thing.

Her doorbell rang. She waited for Natasha to answer it and then remembered the girl had said something about going clubbing up in Birmingham. Then she grinned. Probably that Raisin female. Charles would have phoned her.

She got out of bed and put on her dressing gown and slippers and made her way down to the front door of the manor. The bell rang again. 'I'm coming!' she shouted.

She switched off the burglar alarm and unlocked the door and slid back the bolts. The night had turned chilly and the slush was beginning to freeze. There was no one there. She stepped outside and looked down the drive and then to the right and left. Nothing moved in the stillness of the night.

'Probably kids,' she muttered. But she went back inside and picked up a powerful torch. She went out again and shone the torch round and about, in case any children were hiding in the bushes on either side of the drive. An owl hooted mournfully.

Miriam went back inside. She reset the alarm and made her way back to bed. She was about to pick up her book and resume her reading when the light went out. Miriam groped her way to the bedroom door and pressed down the switch of the overhead light. Nothing.

Odley Cruesis had suffered from occasional power cuts in the past. But she decided she'd better go downstairs to the fuse box and make sure the trip switch was on. Wishing she had brought her torch upstairs with her, she groped her way down to the hall where she had left the torch but could not find it. There were candles in the kitchen. She made her way there. Moonlight was flooding the kitchen. She opened the drawer where she kept candles and matches and lit one of the candles. Holding the candle in one hand, she reached up and opened the fuse box. A heavy blow struck her on the back of the head. The candle flew out of her hand and landed in a pan of fat on the stove.

The maid saw the glow in the sky as she drove down into Odley Cruesis. A fire engine raced past her and then another. When she turned into the manor drive, she could see the house was in flames from top to bottom. Natasha did a U-turn and sped off. She had planned to tell Miriam in the morning that she was leaving. She was an illegal alien from Albania and she knew the police would soon ferret out that fact. They had not seemed to be much interested in her after the murder of John Sunday, but she knew they would focus on her now. She had all her belongings packed up in the battered old Ford Miriam had bought for her. Her real name was Blerta, but Miriam had said, 'I suppose you're called Natasha,' and Blerta had agreed. As she was sure Miriam suspected her of being an illegal alien, she had agreed to low wages and to wearing a maid's uniform. Blerta decided to head back to Birmingham to stay with friends.

In her panic, she did not realize that her running away would make her an arson suspect.

Toni worked at clearing up her flat after Sharon had left. She guiltily wished Agatha had not been so high-handed. Toni was fond of Sharon. Sharon was everything Toni was not – bold and brassy and confident, moving gaily from one boyfriend to another while Toni read books and dreamed of romance.

She felt uneasy. She had visited a club a week before with Sharon and Sharon had been flirting with a group of bikers. They swore a lot and drank a lot and Toni had left early. She hoped Sharon hadn't been getting into bad company.

Agatha was not pleased when she got home to find Charles waiting for her. She was tired and wanted to eat something and go to bed. She only brightened up when Charles told her the full story of his dinner. 'Serves you right,' she said heartlessly. 'You met your match in that cheapskate.'

'There's another thing,' said Charles. 'I've just let the cats out in the garden and there's a glow in the sky from the direction of Odley Cruesis.'

Agatha opened the garden door and went out. Yes, there was a red glow in the sky.

She went back into the kitchen. 'Something's up. I'd better get over there.'

'I'll drive,' said Charles.

As Agatha was about to get into his car, he removed a foil-covered package from the passenger seat.

'You never did!' exclaimed Agatha, smelling fish.

'Oh, yes I did. I paid for it and I wasn't going to let a plate of turbot go to waste.'

They arrived at the manor just in time to see the roof fall in from their vantage point on top of a wall bordering the grounds of the manor.

They couldn't get any nearer because of police and firemen. 'She told me she knew something,' said Charles. 'She told me she had something. She said it seemed impossible and then she said she was going to cancel your services.'

'I wonder if she escaped the fire. And what about the maid?'

'She's gone,' said a voice below them. Agatha got down from the wall, registering that her arthritic hip felt fine although she had been warned that she could not have any more injections and would soon need to have an operation.

The vicar's wife, Penelope, stood there, huddled in an old tweed coat. 'I was coming along the road when her car went past me speeding in the opposite direction. I've told the police. They've set up roadblocks. But I told them she couldn't have anything to do with the fire because as I was walking along, I saw her drive up before she turned around and drove away again.'

'I wonder who benefits from her death, if she's dead,' said Charles. 'She'd been married three times.'

'I think she mentioned a son and daughter.'

'That's right,' said Carrie Brother, joining them. 'Said they were both in America.'

Charles stifled a yawn. 'Come on, Aggie. They're not going to let us get nearer or give us any information tonight.'

Chapter Four

Agatha, who liked watching fictional forensic pro-
grammes on the television, was often amazed at how
slow the real-life forensic process was. Christmas came
and went. She spent a solitary Christmas, persuading
herself that it was just another day. Then came a blustery January, an icy February and so into March and the
timid beginning of the English spring.

In January, she had endured that long overdue hip
operation. Thanks to her active life, she made a speedy
recovery, but then put the whole business of the operation out of her mind. She did not want to admit, even to
herself, that she had needed it. The very words 'hip
operation' screamed *old*.

Patrick Mulligan reported from his sources that
Miriam Courtney had been killed by a blow to the head
with something like a hammer. The fire investigators
found that the electricity had been switched off. The fire
had started at the Aga cooker in the kitchen.

There was no sign of forced entry. The maid had been
found, questioned, cleared of suspicion and deported.
Agatha had been very busy with other cases and her
interest in the case had died, mainly for monetary

reasons. No one was paying her to investigate, Britain was in a recession, and the agency needed all the paying cases they could get.

On a blustery Sunday in late March, when the Cotswolds were full of more daffodils than anyone could remember having seen before, she opened her door and found a tall, handsome man standing on her doorstep. Agatha was immediately aware of the fact that she hadn't a bit of make-up on.

'Mrs Raisin?'

'Yes. You are . . . ?'

'I'm Tom Courtney, Miriam's son.'

'Do come in.' Agatha stood aside to let him past. 'Go straight through to the kitchen.' Agatha did not want to put her guest in the living room because the chairs were soft and she found it awkward to struggle out of them.

'You have a charming cottage,' he said.

He was tall with a lightly tanned face, black hair and brown eyes. Agatha guessed his age to be somewhere in his early forties.

'Do sit down,' said Agatha. 'I am sorry for your loss.'

'Don't be. I was very close to my father, but I didn't see much of my mother.'

'You live in the States now?'

'Yes, in New York.'

'I believe you have a sister.'

'Amy. She's still in the States. She's married to a doctor in Philadelphia.'

'I didn't see either of you at the funeral,' said Agatha.

'I couldn't bring myself to come over. I paid for it, of course, and made the arrangements long distance.'

'Dear me. Why did you dislike your mother so much?'

He shrugged. 'She bitched my poor father to hell and gone. He died of a heart attack when we were small. Amy and I were brought up by a succession of nannies and then we were both sent to schools in Switzerland. Then universities in the States. We went home as little as possible. Believe me, it was a relief when she moved over here. I work as a lawyer.'

'So why have you come to see me?'

'Unfinished business. My mother left everything to Amy and me. Quite a lot. She was a bit of a miser. Not on the big things like expensive schools for us and so on but on niggling things like cheap meals or eating at other people's expense as much as possible, things like that. But I really want to know who killed her and then I can get on with my life. I heard that she had hired you to find out who murdered John Sunday. I would like to hire you to find out who killed my mother.'

'I'll do my best,' said Agatha. 'I feel if I could find out who murdered John Sunday, then I would find out who murdered your mother. She said to a friend of mine the night she was murdered that she knew something.'

He smiled at her, a charming smile that lit up his handsome face. Agatha was even more painfully aware of the fact that not only did she have no make-up on but that she was wearing a tent-like blouse, a cotton skirt and slippers.

'Would you excuse me a moment?' she said hurriedly. She eased herself to her feet, always dimly afraid that the terrible hip pain would come back.

'Hip replacement?' he asked sympathetically.

'No!' lied Agatha. 'Just took a tumble.' Hip replacement, indeed. So aging.

Upstairs, she carefully made up her face and brushed her hair until it shone. She was just struggling into a trouser suit when her doorbell rang. Tom shouted from downstairs, 'Don't worry. I'll get it.'

As she finally made her way downstairs, she could hear laughter from the kitchen. She opened the kitchen door and went in. Toni was sitting at the table facing Tom. Her blonde hair had been newly cut in a short elfin style, making her eyes look large. She was wearing jeans and half boots with a black sweater. A scarlet Puffa jacket hung over the back of her chair.

'Can I help you?' Toni jumped to her feet. 'How's the hip replacement? Healing up okay?'

'What hip replacement?' said Agatha repressively. 'Let's talk about something else. I gather you've introduced yourselves.'

'Indeed,' said Tom in his almost accentless English. 'I didn't know detectives were that pretty off the television screen.'

'You don't have an American accent,' said Toni.

'As I was explaining to Mrs Raisin here, I was schooled in Switzerland so I missed out on the American accent.'

'Mr Courtney,' began Agatha.

'Tom, please.'

'Right. I'm Agatha. Here's my card. If you call at the office on Monday morning, we'll draw up a contract for you. I'll tell you how far we'd got.'

Agatha succinctly outlined all the interviews. When

56

she had finished, Toni said, 'You've forgotten the Beagles and the Summers. You sent me to interview them.'

'Right. But as I remember you didn't get much.'

'They were all so old and creaky.'

Tom smiled. 'Are you very sure? I remember at your age that people like me and Agatha here would seem creaky.'

I'd like to throw something, thought Agatha savagely.

'Oh, *no*,' said Toni, charmingly flustered. 'I mean, neither you nor Agatha are *old*.'

'Bless the girl,' laughed Tom.

'Had they put the Christmas lights up?' asked Agatha. She turned to Tom. 'You see, each Christmas their cottages were blazing with Christmas lights and John Sunday stopped them last Christmas. They were furious. Did they put the lights up after he was murdered, Toni?'

'They hadn't done when I called on them and then I never went back to Odley Cruesis.'

'Will you rebuild the manor?' Agatha asked Tom.

'No, I'm selling the wreck to a builder. He's going to bulldoze the ruin and then build houses on the land.'

'Was the place insured?'

'Yes, heavily.'

Agatha asked, 'Have the police inquired where you were the night your mother was murdered?'

'Of course. I was in the Cayman Islands on holiday. Plenty of witnesses.'

The doorbell rang again. 'You're a busy lady,' commented Tom.

'I'll get it,' said Toni. She came back followed by Roy Silver. Roy had once worked for Agatha when she had run her own public relations firm. He was still in PR. As a concession to a visit to the countryside, Roy was wearing a sports jacket, but underneath he sported a T-shirt with the logo Ready To Kill. He was a rather weedy young man with a weak pale face and fine hair, cut short and gelled into small spikes all over his narrow head.

'Aggie, darling,' he said, kissing her on the cheek. 'I'll just pop my bag in the spare room.'

Agatha caught an amused look in Tom's eyes and said hurriedly, 'My young friend used to work for me. You might have phoned, Roy.'

'Came on an impulse. Read about all the Cotswolds mayhem in the papers and then nothing. I thought you might have asked me for Christmas. There I was on my little own.'

'I assumed everyone I knew would be booked up for Christmas,' said Agatha defensively.

Roy went off upstairs. Agatha said, 'I'd like to get back to Odley Cruesis and begin again. I don't like the idea of asking you to work on your day off, Toni. I'll let you know on Monday how I get on.'

'Oh, I'm free,' said Toni blithely.

Agatha silently cursed both Roy and Toni. No chance of being alone with Tom.

When Roy came back downstairs, Agatha said, 'We're going detecting. You can stay here if you like.'

'Dear Aggie, remember all the times I've spent ferreting around with you. Are we going to start today?'

'I'll get my notes,' said Agatha, 'and then we can split up.'

When she returned, she said, 'First of all, Tom, do you want to go back to where you are staying and wait results? Where *are* you staying?'

'At the George in Mircester. But I'd like to come with you.'

Agatha brightened. She consulted her notes. 'Right. Toni, if you and Roy could go and see Tilly Glossop again, she might open up to you. Tom and I will go and see the Beagles and the Summerses. Probably a waste of time but I would like to see them for myself.' The doorbell shrilled.

'Don't move. I'll get it.' Toni ran to the door.

She came back with Mrs Bloxby. 'I hadn't seen you for a while,' said the vicar's wife, 'and wondered how you were getting on.'

Agatha, who did not want another remark about her hip, flashed her friend a warning look. Mrs Bloxby focused on Tom for the first time. Agatha introduced them.

She's off again, thought Mrs Bloxby. I should be worried about her, but she needed some man to bring the sparkle back.

'We're all going detecting,' said Agatha.

'In that case, I won't keep you,' said Mrs Bloxby. 'But why don't you all call at the vicarage for tea later and let me know how you get on?'

Agatha elected to drive after a look at Tom's vehicle. It was a Range Rover and she cringed at the thought of climbing up into it. The day was still fine: blue sky, yellow daffodils, pink cherry blossoms and some purple stuff that Agatha didn't know the name of growing out of the old Cotswold walls.

'Young Roy seems a close friend of yours,' said Tom.

'I suppose he is.'

'Aren't you frightened of getting AIDS?'

Agatha nearly swerved into a ditch. She stopped the car and said in a thin voice, 'I am not having an affair with Roy. I do not know whether he is homosexual or not. I never asked, it being none of my business, but it wouldn't matter if he were.'

'But the close contact?' said Tom.

Agatha glared at him. 'Are you one of those freaks who think you can get it from lavatory seats?'

'Sorry,' mumbled Tom. 'I didn't take you for a liberal.'

'You see before you,' said Agatha, 'an apolitical woman with a lot of common sense who doesn't listen to folk stories or ill-informed scares. Now, can we get on?'

They drove on in silence, Agatha's interest in Tom extinguished. As they were driving into Odley Cruesis, Tom said, 'Maybe I shouldn't have said that. I lost a good friend to AIDS.'

'What happened?' asked Agatha acidly. 'Did her boyfriend breathe on her?'

'Him. He died. It was awful. I've been frightened of that horrible disease ever since.'

'Ah, that explains it,' said Agatha, suddenly cheerful again. 'Here we are. I think the Beagles are in the first cottage.'

The cottage had probably once been a farm labourer's cottage. It was made of red brick with a slate roof. The path up to the front door was of red brick as well. A glorious magnolia tree was just coming into flower in the little front garden.

Agatha rang the bell. An elderly man answered the door. He was small and round-shouldered, wearing two pullovers over a frayed shirt and baggy stained trousers. His face was wrinkled. Spare lines of greased hair covered a freckled scalp. His faded blue eyes looked at Agatha. 'So it's you. Nosey parker.'

'This is Thomas Courtney, Miriam's son,' said Agatha.

'Oh, I do be right sorry. Come along in. The missus is poorly today.'

'What's up with her?' asked Tom sharply.

'Her do have a bit of a cold.'

'I might wait in the car,' said Tom nervously.

'It's just a cold!' exclaimed Agatha. 'Not the black plague.'

'Very well,' he said reluctantly.

Mrs Beagle was crouched in an armchair beside the fire. The room smelled strongly of urine, coal smoke and wintergreen.

'Here's Miriam's boy,' said her husband.

Mrs Beagle was as wrapped up as her husband and every bit as stooped and wrinkled. Agatha mentally removed them from her list of suspects. She estimated they would both have difficulty getting across the street, let alone murdering John Sunday.

Agatha looked around her, but there was nowhere in the small parlour to sit down. Charlie Beagle had sunk down into an armchair facing his wife. There was a battered sofa but two large somnolent dogs were stretched out on it.

'Did you see anyone near the manor before it went alight?' asked Agatha.

'In the middle of the night!' said Charlie. 'Us were asleep. Didn't hear about it till morning.'

'About John Sunday,' pursued Agatha, 'you were at that protest meeting.'

'And a fat lot of good that did,' said Mrs Beagle. 'Jabber, jabber, talk, talk. Nothing could be done about that horrible man.'

'Apart from Miriam and Miss Simms, did anyone else leave the room?'

'Not that I noticed,' said Charlie. 'But me and the missus, our sight isn't as good as it used to be. But good riddance to Sunday, I say. He was after stopping us putting up the Christmas lights. Such a display we had every year. We was in the *Cotswold Journal.* I'll show you. They sent me a photo and Fred Summer got one as well.'

He shuffled over to a table by the window, piled high with magazines, newspapers and photos.

'Here we are. Just you look at that!'

Agatha studied a colour photograph showing the two cottages. The outsides were covered with Christmas lights. The Summers had a plastic Santa and plastic reindeer riding on the roof and the Beagles had a lit-up plastic crèche in their front garden. Perhaps the only thing John Sunday did in his life that became it, thought Agatha, who had seen a performance of *Macbeth* once, was blacking out this monstrosity.

Then her bearlike eyes narrowed. Surely Charlie couldn't be that infirm if he had got the plastic Santa up on the roof, not to mention wiring up all those lights.

'What a lot of work,' she said. 'It must have taken you ages.'

'I starts around the end of October, yes. Bit by bit.'

'And did you get that Santa up on the roof all by yourself?'

'Easy. There's a skylight. I just push it up through there.'

'Do you want to ask anything?' Agatha turned to Tom, who was standing with a handkerchief covering his mouth and nose.

He gave a muffled 'No.'

They took their leave. 'You really are terrified of infection,' said Agatha when they were outside.

'I hate colds.'

'I don't think there's much point in interviewing the Summers,' said Agatha. 'On the other hand, they might have seen something.'

'Do you mind if I wait outside?'

'Not at all,' said Agatha, her interest in him dying by the minute.

The Summers seemed mirror images of the Beagles, except that Fred Summer looked fitter. His wife also had a cold and was coughing miserably. Agatha felt the air was full of germs and began to sympathize with Tom.

Fred's story was almost the same as that of Charles Beagle. They had visited the vicarage, more in the hope of some cakes and tea than out of any hope that something about Sunday might be resolved. There was one piece of additional information. Fred and Charlie used to compete to see which one of them could have the most dazzling display at Christmas, but as they both got older, they had begun to help each other.

Agatha thanked them and left. Tom was standing outside, a light breeze ruffling his hair. He looked so handsome that Agatha felt a lurch in her stomach. It suddenly seemed a long time since she had enjoyed any sex whatsoever, and she felt her hormones raging.

Toni and Roy came rushing up to join them. Toni looked excited. 'Tilly Glossop was out,' she said, 'but her neighbour, a Mrs Crinch, came out to talk to us. She does not like Tilly. She said that Sunday was a frequent visitor but that the day before the murder, she heard Sunday and Tilly having a terrible row. When he left Tilly's cottage, Sunday shouted, "Get it through your head, we're finished." To which Tilly said, "You'll be sorry."'

'I think what we should do,' said Agatha, 'is accept Mrs Bloxby's offer of tea and go through what we've got. We'll need to dig up all we can about Tilly.'

Mrs Bloxby suggested they should take their tea in the garden as the day was fine and it would give Mrs Raisin a chance to smoke.

'You *smoke*!' exclaimed Tom. 'Don't you know what you are doing to your lungs? And what about other people? Have you never heard of passive smoking?'

'We are out in the open air,' said Agatha huffily as they helped Mrs Bloxby to arrange chairs round the table in the garden.

Mrs Bloxby watched the emotions chasing each other across Agatha's face as she looked at Tom: an odd mixture of exasperation, disappointment and lust. Odd, thought Mrs Bloxby, I never thought of Mrs Raisin as a *lustful* person – more of a romantic. Does she not realize that inside that handsome exterior is probably a very prissy man? Just look at the way he is polishing that already clean seat with his handkerchief.

Toni and Roy arrived to join them, saying they had not been able to find Tilly Glossop and all the other villagers had shunned them as if they had the plague.

After tea and cakes had been served, Mrs Bloxby asked how they were getting on. Agatha outlined the little they had found. When she had finished, she said, 'I don't know what's happened to Bill Wong. He usually calls round. I thought that after the death of Sunday he would come to see me. I tried phoning but he is always busy.'

'Oh, I quite forgot to tell you!' exclaimed Mrs Bloxby. 'He called me on the telephone some time ago, saying that Detective Sergeant Collins watches him like a hawk and Wilkes said he was to give you no help whatsoever because he did not want outsiders meddling in police work.'

'Considering the crimes I've solved for the police in the past, I do think that's a bit thick,' said Agatha. 'I might drive over later and see if he's at home. Have you heard any gossip about Tilly Glossop?'

'Only that she is not very well liked. There are remarkably few newcomers in Odley Cruesis, compared to the other villages, but such as they are complain that she is very rude to them. May Dinwoody and Carrie Brother are quite popular. Miss Brother is considered an eccentric. What makes you think that the death of Mrs Courtney and the death of Mr Sunday are connected?'

'It stands to reason,' said Agatha. 'She told Charles she had remembered something. Miriam probably told whoever it was and they decided to kill her.'

'But the killing of Mrs Courtney was quite elaborate,' said Toni, 'whereas the killing of John Sunday looks more as if someone just stabbed him in a rage.'

Tom gave a laugh. 'It's a good thing I have a solid alibi or I would be number one suspect.' He took a packet of moist disinfectant tissues out of his pocket and began to clean his hands.

Agatha gave a little sigh. There he sat, the epitome of manhood with his handsome face, his strong throat and his strong figure, fussing away like an old woman.

'Where are you staying, Mr Courtney?' asked Mrs Bloxby.

'At the George in Mircester.'

'Do you plan to stay long?'

'Just until all the legal business is settled. Pretty nearly finished. I should be off back to the States in a week or two.'

'I heard you have a sister,' said Mrs Bloxby.

66

'Yes, Amy. She's leaving all the business side of things to me. Mother left everything equally to the two of us.'

'Her death must have come as a terrible shock to you both.'

'Well, ma'am, it did and then it didn't. Mother had a bad knack of rubbing people up the wrong way.'

'But surely she cannot have been the type of lady to drive anyone to murder!'

'To tell you the truth, I've been racking my brains and cannot really think of anyone,' said Tom ruefully.

Agatha wondered why Roy, usually a chatterbox, was so silent. She looked across at him and saw he had fallen asleep, the spring sunlight bathing his thin face. For the first time, Agatha wondered why he had come on a visit without phoning first. He had only done that before when he was in some sort of trouble.

'Roy!' she said sharply.

'Eh, what?'

'I'm going to drive into Mircester to try to have a word with Bill. Want to come?'

Roy straightened up and rubbed his eyes. 'Right you are.'

'Perhaps we could all meet at my hotel for dinner tonight. Eight o'clock?' said Tom.

'I can't,' said Toni. 'I promised Sharon I'd go to a disco with her.'

'And I, alas, have parish duties,' said Mrs Bloxby.

'We'd love to,' said Agatha, wondering if she could persuade Roy to stay in for the evening. Tom was a bit fussy, that was all.

* * *

On the road to Mircester, Agatha said to Roy, 'Out with it.'

'Out with what?'

'I feel something's bothering you.'

'Oh, that,' said Roy bleakly. 'I suppose it's no big deal. It's just that I've lost all interest in the job.'

'Who are you handling at the moment?'

'Paper Panties.'

'I thought those things went out with the sixties.'

'They want them back and I've got to get the media interested.'

'So? You just do your job as usual. You know what it's like, Roy. Remember all the lousy accounts I had to cope with.'

'I don't get on well with foreigners.'

'What kind of foreigners?'

'Bulgarian. The girls are pretty, the ones they get to model the panties. But the people who run the company treat me like dirt. In fact, they're pretty threatening. In fact, they give me the impression that if they don't get maximum coverage, I'll end up off Westminster Bridge.'

'I'm surprised at your boss taking them on.'

'They sent an English rep to the office to set it up. Very correct, upper-class-twit type. I want out of it.'

Agatha furrowed her brow in thought. Then she said, 'Oh, I've got it. Sometime today we'll stop off and get some cheap stationery, put on gloves and send a nice anonymous letter to the vice squad saying it's a front for prostitution and the models are sex slaves.'

'Aggie!'

'Well, think about it. The police will feel compelled to

investigate. You tell your boss that the reputation of his firm is in danger and you'll be off the hook.'

'But forensics!' wailed Roy. 'What if we even *breathe* on the paper!'

'You've been watching too much *CSI* on television. Have I ever let you down?'

'Well . . .'

'Leave it to me.'

They were in luck. Bill Wong's formidable parents were out shopping. Bill's mother was a Gloucestershire woman and his father was originally from Hong Kong. Agatha thought they were both horrible, but Bill adored his parents.

'You've been avoiding me,' accused Agatha when Bill opened the door to them.

'It's Collins. Wilkes wants me to have nothing to do with you and she watches me all the time.'

'Well, she isn't around now,' said Agatha cheerfully. 'Let us in. We need to talk.'

Bill led them into the lounge. There was a new three-piece suite covered in plastic. 'You'd better get that plastic off before the warm weather comes,' commented Agatha, 'or it'll stick like hell.'

'Oh, it'll keep it clean for a bit,' said Bill. 'What's going on?'

'Miriam Courtney's son has arrived. He wants me to find out who killed his mother.'

'Why now?' asked Bill in his soft Gloucestershire accent. He had a pleasant round face with almond-shaped eyes. 'I mean, he didn't even bother to turn up for the funeral. Neither did his sister.'

'It seems as if Miriam had as little to do with them as possible and they didn't like her one little bit. He's over to supervise the selling of the property. That's why he's suddenly turned up.'

'But you would think he would call on the police first before hiring a private detective.'

'I am very good at my job,' said Agatha.

'But people normally only hire a private detective in such circumstances as a last resort. They question the police first.'

'*Have* you got anything?' asked Agatha.

'No, and we've tried and tried. It's a very close-knit village. Take the case of John Sunday. He was so unpopular all round that any number of people could have wanted him dead.'

'Tilly Glossop in particular,' said Agatha, and told him Toni's news.

'We've interrogated her several times,' said Bill. 'Saying to someone, "You'll be sorry," is hardly a reason to arrest them.'

'And Tom Courtney was definitely in the Cayman Islands?'

'Yes.'

'And the sister?'

'In Philadelphia. She's married to a Dr Bairns.'

'And the doctor vouches for her?'

'He was away at a medical conference in Seattle. But she was staying with a friend, Harriet Temple. Believe me, they were checked out. And Miriam did tell Charles that she was on to something. And before she went to bed on the night she was killed, she phoned the vicar's wife and said she knew who had done it.'

'I didn't know that,' said Agatha excitedly. 'That could mean either Penelope or her husband did it.'

'Of course we thought of that. But Mrs Timson's cleaner was ill and she phoned her to see how she was getting on and told her what Miriam had said. The cleaner, a Mrs Radley, promptly got on the phone to a lot of people in the village. We questioned them all. But the ones she called had in their turn called others. Everyone must have known.'

'It's a puzzle,' sighed Agatha. 'The two murders seem so different. The killing of John Sunday almost seems like a spur-of-the-moment thing, whereas the murder of Miriam looks like cold-blooded planning.'

'That's a leap in the dark,' said Bill, 'and it doesn't add up. She tells Charles she's on to something and the next thing, she's dead. Sherry?'

'Please,' said Roy, who had been wondering whether to tell Bill about Agatha's mad idea of how to get him away from the Bulgarians.

Bill went through to the kitchen and reappeared with a little silver tray holding three minuscule glasses of sherry. Roy's face fell. He knew Agatha would not want him to tell Bill about her plans for the Bulgarians but felt that a stiff drink might have given him the necessary courage.

'I think Tom Courtney looks suspicious,' said Roy. 'I mean, the motive is usually money, isn't it?'

'The first thing we thought of, but, like I said, his alibi checks out. And the sister is vouched for by her friend.'

'It's a pity,' mused Agatha, 'that it couldn't be either the son or daughter. I mean, how convenient to already have a murder in the village. The police were bound to think both murders were connected.'

'We still do,' said Bill. 'You're right, though: the murder of Miriam appears to have been carefully planned. Someone passing the manor saw the lights go out and then the flickering light of a candle, as if Miriam was going down the stairs to look at the fuse box. The fire was started because when she was struck down, the candle she might have been holding ended up in a pan of fat.'

'Can they tell all that? The house was a blazing inferno. I didn't think there would be any evidence left.'

'They traced the source of the fire to the stove, analysed the remains of the pan and found evidence of candle grease. The fuse box was nearly intact, being protected by a heavy metal cover. The electricity had definitely been switched off.'

'Who was it who was just passing so late at night?'

'Carrie Brother.'

'And what's her reason for being out so late?'

'She said her little doggie needed to go pee-pee, to quote her words.'

'I think she's barmy,' said Agatha.

Bill shook his head. 'A bit eccentric, that's all. Is it any use, Agatha, telling you yet again to keep out of it?'

'Not in the slightest. I'm employed by Tom Courtney and I need the money.'

'Do you know anything about Bulgarians in London?' asked Roy.

'No, he doesn't,' said Agatha. 'We've got to rush. Come along, Roy.'

Roy quailed before the gimlet gleam in Agatha's bear-like eyes. 'What Bulgarians?' asked Bill as Agatha hustled Roy out of the house.

'Never mind,' Agatha called back.

Back in Carsely, Roy wandered around the cottage moodily while Agatha composed an anonymous letter to the police. Finally she popped the letter in an envelope. 'I'd better not mail this here,' she muttered. 'If they see a Carsely postmark, they'll track me down. Roy!' she called.

'What is it?' he asked nervously.

'I want you to mail this in London. I'll put it in a bigger envelope so you don't get your fingerprints on it. Just take it out and pop it in a pillar-box.' She stripped off her gloves and then noticed the look of relief in Roy's eyes. 'And don't think you can tear it up and chuck it away when you get to London. If I don't see anything in the news about a raid, I'll know you've weaselled out. It's for your own good! Now, I would like to have dinner with Tom on my own this evening. I think he rather fancies me and I may get more out of him. He might remember something about his mother that he hasn't told me.'

'He doesn't fancy you a bit,' said Roy crossly. 'I'm your friend. You should be looking after me.'

'Roy, it's work. We're in the middle of a recession and I need this job.'

'Oh, all right,' said Roy. 'I'll maybe go to the pub.'

That evening, after Agatha had departed in a wave of French perfume, Roy, restless, decided to drive over to Odley Cruesis. He fancied himself as a detective. Maybe if he found out something significant, Agatha would offer him a job and he could escape the PR business.

He drove off through the leafy lanes with the car window open, breathing in the scents of the country evening. He noticed there were lights on in the church hall, a square building next to the old Norman church. Roy parked the car and went into the hall. A bingo session was underway. Villagers were crouched over their cards while Penelope Timson read out the numbers in a high strangulated voice.

Roy took a seat at the back of the hall. When Penelope finally called a break for refreshment and everyone rose to hurry over to a side table where there was a tea urn and plates piled high with sandwiches and cakes, Roy had a brilliant idea. He was addicted to watching the television series *Poirot*, based on the books of Agatha Christie. He particularly liked the bit where the great detective accused one after the other in the last scene before unmasking the murderer. He ran quickly up to the microphone and called out, 'Your attention, please!'

Faces turned towards him. 'I am Roy Silver,' he announced, 'and I am investigating these murders. I know who did it. I shall wait outside. All the guilty person has to do is come to me and confess. I will intercede with the police to help ease the sentence. Thank you.'

Roy left the hall amid a startled silence. As he waited outside, he was very pleased with himself. Of course he didn't expect the murderer to approach him. But he did expect the villagers to crowd round him and discuss the murders. Maybe he could pick up some information that Agatha had missed.

After half an hour, he could hear Penelope's voice inside the hall once more raised as she called out the bingo numbers.

He was beginning to feel silly, but decided to wait on. He stood beside his car in the darkness. The village had gone 'green' by opting to have the street lights switched off. The silhouettes of the old cottages crouched around him in the dark, hunched and sinister.

Roy doggedly waited for the bingo session to finish. At last it was over and they all filed out. No one spoke. Not even to each other. They spread out towards their various homes as if he didn't exist. When the last one had gone and he saw Penelope locking up the hall, he approached her. 'Mrs Timson!'

She started and swung round. Penelope looked at him severely. 'That was a silly joke.'

'Wasn't a joke,' protested Roy shrilly.

'Oh, just leave, young man,' said Penelope wearily.

Roy walked slowly back to his car. A small moon was riding high above, casting black shadows across the road in front of him. A breeze had risen and the sounds of it in the leaves of the trees sounded like whispering, menacing voices. He gave himself a shake. The country life was definitely not for him.

A savage blow from behind struck him on the back of the head. He fell forwards. As he fell, his fluorescent phone slipped out of his jacket pocket and lay on the road in front of his dimming eyes. With his last bit of strength, he pressed the number three, where he had Agatha's phone number logged. 'Get help,' he croaked. 'Murdered.' And then he lost consciousness.

Tilly Glossop phoned Mrs Timson. 'That peculiar young man is lying on the road beside his car. Do you think there's something up with him?'

'Drunk,' said the vicar's wife succinctly. 'Leave him to sleep it off.'

Agatha was aglow with alcohol and lust. Tom had paid her many compliments so that she felt young and attractive again.

Over coffee, he said, 'I have some very good brandy in my room. Why don't we go up there?'

This is it, thought Agatha. Now or never. Just once, just once, before I'm very old. Take mental inventory. Legs shaved, armpits ditto. Should she have got a Brazilian? Too late now.

When they entered his hotel room, she did wish he would just take her in his arms and kiss her. He poured her a measure of brandy and then one for himself and sat next to her on a slippery sofa in the small sitting room of his suite. He smiled. 'To us and to the night ahead.' They clinked glasses.

'I do like to get certain things out of the way first,' he said. 'Have you ever had any sexually transmitted diseases?'

Agatha looked at him with eyes of stone. 'Anything else or do you have a very long catalogue?'

He grinned boyishly. 'Don't know how it is, but I never could bear pubic hair on a woman.'

'Neither can a paedophile. Listen, Tom, this is one horrible mistake. If you want to lay down terms like this, I suggest you go somewhere and pay for it. Now, if you don't mind—'

Her mobile rang. She was later to thank God for the crassness of Tom's approach or she might never have answered it. She listened in alarm to Roy's message.

'It's Roy! He's hurt.'

She called the police, she called the ambulance, and then got to her feet and hurried to the door. 'You've been drinking. You can't drive,' exclaimed Tom.

'Oh, bug off,' hissed Agatha and ran out of the room.

When Agatha got to Odley Cruesis, she saw the police were already there and Roy was being loaded into an ambulance. She saw Bill Wong and hurried towards him. 'Is Roy alive?'

'Just. It's a bad blow.'

'I'll go in the ambulance with him.'

'Agatha, you've been drinking.'

'So what? I'm not going to drive the ambulance.'

Agatha waited miserably at the hospital and was soon joined by Toni and Sharon. Bill had phoned Toni. 'Any idea who did this?' asked Agatha.

Toni shook her head. 'But it seems that Roy went to a bingo meeting at the village hall and claimed he knew the identity of the murderer and the murderer should speak to him outside and confess all.'

'I should never have given him that boxed set of *Poirot* for Christmas,' mourned Agatha. 'What on earth came over him? And which of the murders was he talking about? It must be the first one because he knew I was having dinner with Tom.'

'Here's Bill,' said Sharon.

'It's bad,' said Bill. 'There's bleeding in the brain. They're operating now. You may as well all go home. There's nothing more you can do here.'

'Will he live?'

'They don't know. But evidently, for such a weak-looking fellow, he's got a skull like iron and that might save him.'

'Didn't anyone see anything?'

Bill told her about the call to the vicar's wife.

'But that's ridiculous!' exclaimed Agatha. 'Roy tells them he knows the identity of the murderer, then he's reported lying on the road and no one thinks they should go and have a look at him?'

'According to village report, they estimate he was drunk and sleeping it off.'

'Any idea what struck him?'

'Blunt instrument. Maybe a hammer. I don't like Sergeant Collins but I was glad of her because she ripped into all these villagers, banging on doors, waking them up, shouting at them – it would have done your heart glad, Agatha. Now, go home.'

'Maybe I can sit by his bed,' pleaded Agatha, 'and, you know, talk to him.'

'Agatha, it's not a soap. He's not in a coma. He's under anaesthetic on an operating table getting a couple of holes drilled in his head. You'll maybe be able to see him in the morning. Go home and get some sleep.'

Agatha was just wearily climbing into bed when the door opened and Charles strolled in.

'Roy's been hit on the head,' said Agatha. 'He might not live.'

She burst into tears. Charles sat down on the bed and hugged her until she had finished crying. 'Now, tell me all about it.'

So Agatha did. When she had finished, Charles said, 'I've been wondering about Tom Courtney.'

'Why him?' asked Agatha. 'Anyway he was having dinner with me while someone was trying to kill Roy. And why would he want to kill John Sunday?'

'Oh, I just thought that maybe he had already planned to bump off mum and torch the place and wanted Grudge out of the way before any objections to an expensive building site started up. So he was having dinner with you and you're back at dawn still smelling of Mademoiselle Coco. Did you get seduced?'

'The call about Roy interrupted dinner, thank God. Do you know he asked me if I had shaved?'

Charles ran a hand over Agatha's face. 'Smooth as a baby's bum. Oh, you mean the other end. What larks! What a chat-up line!'

'Leave me alone now, Charles. I've set the alarm. I've got to get back to the hospital first thing. And then there's Sharon's eyes.'

'What about them?'

But a gentle snore was the only reply.

Three hours later Agatha was back on the road to Mircester Hospital with Charles driving. 'I don't suppose you want to work for Tom again,' commented Charles. 'Do look at these stupid wood pigeons. All over the road.'

'Not really,' said Agatha. 'But he may be connected to the murders somehow or he may know someone who is. I'll forget about last night and go on as usual.'

'What about Sharon's eyes? You mumbled something before you fell asleep.'

'Oh, that. Maybe it was because we were all so upset last night but the pupils of her eyes looked like pinpricks. I'll get Toni to find out how she's doing.'

'Do you ever think about that jolly fling we had in the south of France?'

Agatha glanced quickly at Charles but his face was calm and neutral.

She manufactured a little laugh. 'From time to time. I was so glad to escape from my dreadful fiancé.' Agatha had been briefly engaged to a villager who had taken her on holiday to Normandy. But he had turned out to be so awful that Agatha had had to phone Charles to come and rescue her. Then she and Charles had driven down to the south of France for a brief holiday.

'And that's all it was?'

'Just the way you put it yourself, dear,' said Agatha in a thin voice. '"Well, that was a bit of fun," you said, "but troubles at home and I've got to dash." Never mind. Let's see how Roy is doing.'

Roy looked like a fledgling abandoned by its mother. His head was shaved on one side. The matron came bustling in. 'Relatives only.'

'Aunt and uncle,' said Agatha. 'How are you doing?' she asked Roy.

'They're ever so pleased with me,' said Roy. 'I've got to rest up for a week and not get on any planes. I've got two holes in my head. Look! I feel like a bowling ball.'

'Whatever possessed you to do such a dangerous thing?' asked Agatha.

'I thought I could stir something up, just like you. Anyway, I phoned Pedmans and they've given the Bulgarian account to Mary.' Mary, a rival public relations officer, was always trying to poach Roy's accounts. 'As soon as I get out of here, I'll hand in my notice.'

'And do what?' asked Charles.

'Don't know. Maybe something in the country. I could work for you, Aggie.'

'It's mostly work out in the countryside and villages, Roy. I always think of you as a town person.'

Roy suddenly remembered the sinister darkness and silence of Odley Cruesis with not even one jolly red London bus to break the brooding fear of the place.

'I'll think of something anyway,' he said brightly. 'Do you know a British surgeon goes out to the Ukraine every year and performs these operations with a Black and Decker electric drill because they haven't the equipment out there?'

Bill Wong and Inspector Wilkes came in to interview Roy, and Agatha and Charles were banished to the waiting room. 'I'll be off,' said Charles. 'See you later.'

Agatha flicked through the glossy pages of a magazine. There were photographs of jolly people at openings of this and that and at hunt dinners. How happy they all look, she thought. How the camera lies. Nothing to show the raving row on the road home or the imminent divorce or the threat of bankruptcy or the social pain because Lady Bollocks-To-You snubbed the garage owner's wife. The magazine slipped from her lap and she fell asleep.

Charles came back late in the afternoon and woke Agatha up. 'You've been asleep for hours,' he said. 'Toni and Sharon have been around and Phil and Patrick. Pedmans has sent a hamper from Fortnum & Mason and

82

everyone seems to be eating bits out of it except Roy. His real uncle and aunt have turned up and are going to take him away tomorrow to look after him. Funny that, I never think of Roy as having any family at all.'

They approached the room but were told by a nurse that Roy was asleep and it would be better to let him rest.

Agatha looked at her watch. 'I'd better get to the office and find out if anyone has discovered anything.'

'See you tomorrow,' said Charles.

She watched his well-tailored back disappear along the corridor. Had that brief fling in the south of France meant anything to him? He had never mentioned it before today. She took a small mirror out of her handbag and squawked in dismay at her face. Her mascara was lying in little black blobs under her eyes in that irritating way that supposedly waterproof mascara is apt to do. It was a magnifying mirror and she felt her pores made her face look like part of the surface of the moon.

By the time she had washed her face and repaired her make-up and had driven to the office, it was to find Mrs Freedman just about to close up and Sharon brushing out her long tresses, blonde streaked with purple.

She told them the latest news of Roy. 'The others are all still over at that terrible village trying to find out something,' said Mrs Freedman. 'Would you like me to stay on?'

'No, you can go. Sharon, I want a word with you.'

Sharon threw down the hairbrush and retreated to her desk. 'What is it now?'

Agatha waited until Mrs Freedman had closed the office door behind her and then said, 'What drugs are you taking?'

'I ain't taking none.'

'Don't lie to me. What is it? Coke, crystal meth, heroin – what?'

'Nothing. Gotta go.'

'The pupils of your eyes are tiny. You're on something. You can't work for me and be on drugs.'

'What about you, you boozy old bat, with your fags and gin?' demanded Sharon. 'Stuff your job.'

Sharon rushed out of the office, leaving only an aroma of sweat and cheap perfume behind her.

Why should I bother? thought Agatha mutinously. I'm not her mother.

When she arrived at her cottage it was to find a large bouquet of pink roses on the kitchen table with a note from Doris, which read, 'These arrived today. Got yourself a fellow?'

Agatha read the card attached to the roses. 'Don't be mad at me. Love, Tom.'

Freak, thought Agatha bitterly. She fed her cats and then carried the bunch of roses up to the vicarage. 'These might look nice in the church,' said Agatha, handing them to Mrs Bloxby.

'How kind of you!'

'I'm afraid kindness doesn't enter into it. I'm getting rid of them.'

'Come in anyway. We'll have coffee. How is Roy? I heard it all on the news.'

'He's recovering all right.'

Agatha sank down wearily into the feathered cushions on the old vicarage sofa. 'The flowers are from Tom Courtney. He took me out to dinner last night. He asked me if I had any sexually transmitted diseases and then he asked me if I had shaved.'

'*Shaved*? Oh, I see.' The vicar's wife turned a little pink. 'I never will understand the lack of romance in this modern age. We get a lot of couples coming to the vicarage for advice on marriage. They only do it, mainly, because the girl wants a church wedding and usually they've never been near the place since they were baptized. There was one young man who said to his fiancée in front of Alf, "We're going to Antigua on our honeymoon so she'd better get to one of those tanning parlours and get an all-over tan. Don't want her looking like a shark's belly on the beach." It seems men can make *demands* these days and without even paying for it like the days when they had to go to a brothel.'

'Nothing like the good old days,' giggled Agatha.

'Well, no romance like there used to be. Nothing like a bit of frustration for engendering romance. You're surely not still going to go on working for him?'

'Sure. Money's short these days and he pays generously. It's funny. I have a gut feeling that Tom Courtney is the sort who might be capable of murdering his own mother, but he's got such a cast-iron alibi. I wonder, too, about that sister of his. I mean she could have got her friend to swear she was there at the time of the murder. Oh, I forgot. There's no record of her entering the UK.'

'There is such a great deal of money involved,' said Mrs Bloxby.

'They could have paid someone,' said Agatha slowly. 'I've a good mind to nip over to Philadelphia and take a look around. I know, I'll go back and see Roy and get him to put it about that I'm taking him off to a health resort and I'll be back in a few days.'

Roy was sitting up in bed, eating grapes from a huge basket of fruit on the table beside his bed. 'Guess who's just been to see me, Aggie?'

'The fruit fairy?'

'Mr Pedman himself! He brought me all that lovely fruit. Do you remember that idea of mine of sending an anonymous letter to the police saying the Bulgarians were into sex trafficking?'

'My idea, actually.'

'Whatever. Anyway, it turns out to be true. Drugs as well as girls. Bitch, Mary, had been singing their praises and said I had only been reluctant to work for the vulgar Bulgars because I was running out of steam. She is *definitely* not the flavour of the month. I'm getting a raise in pay!'

'Okay. In return for my help – *my* help, mind – I want you to do something for me. Tell everyone who calls on you, including Bill – *especially* Bill – that I've gone off to a health farm for a few days and, no, you don't know which one.'

'Do you want to see my picture in the local paper?'

'No, Narcissus. I'm off.'

Chapter Five

Agatha was feeling very low as it was announced that the plane was approaching Philadelphia. She had begun to question her own motives in taking this expensive trip. What did she know of men these days? Maybe they all went around asking intimate questions before they'd even opened the bedroom door. It had been a gut conviction that there was something seriously weird about Tom Courtney that had driven her on. Alibis had been checked by the police on both sides of the Atlantic. What on earth did she expect to find out?

Once through immigration, she took out the Google maps she had run off her computer before leaving and asked a taxi driver to take her to Sellivex Drive, home of Dr and Mrs Bairns.

What if they're not at home? fretted Agatha as the taxi eventually swung round into a leafy drive. She asked the driver if he would wait. 'Sure thing, lady,' he said. 'But pay this part first.'

Agatha did, and added a generous tip.

The house was pseudo-colonial, built of red brick and with white columns at the entrance. Manicured lawns separated it from its identical neighbours on either side. No children played.

Agatha went up the red-brick path which ran along the right side of the lawn, past a garage pretending to be a stables, with a brass horse on the roof, and so round to the door.

She pressed the doorbell. A voice from inside called out, 'See who that is, Sally.'

The door opened. A stout woman with grey hair stood there. 'Yes?'

Agatha presented her card. 'Mrs Bairns, please.'

'Just you wait heah.'

Agatha waited.

After a few moments, Sally reappeared. 'Step this way, ma'am. Remove your shoes first.'

Agatha walked into a blast of freezing air-conditioning and through to a large, spacious room furnished with very little indeed. The Bairns family seemed to prefer minimalism. The walls were white. The paintings seemed to be totally black. There were only three leather chairs with spindly steel legs in the room and one black marble coffee table.

Mrs Amy Bairns remained seated. She was a tall blonde with that Californian face-lift look which makes a lot of face-lifted women look the same – like creatures from the Planet Botox.

She did not smile. Probably would crack her face if she did, thought Agatha.

'How can I help you?' asked Amy. Agatha sat down.

'Tom Courtney has asked me to help find out who murdered your mother,' began Agatha.

'So what brings you here?'

'As you are his sister, I thought you might remember something, something that might give me a clue as to who might want your mother dead. Did she have any enemies?'

'Mother was not popular. But, no, no one hated her enough to kill her.'

'Perhaps I might have a word with your friend, Harriet Temple.'

'Are you trying to tell me you *dare* to doubt my alibi?'

'No, nothing like that. But she may remember something about Mrs Courtney.'

'She barely knew Mother. Now, my time is valuable even if yours is not.' Amy must have pressed a hidden bell somewhere because Sally promptly appeared.

'Mrs Raisin is just leaving.'

Agatha threw her a baffled look. Why such animosity when all she was doing was trying to find out who had murdered the woman's mother?

She followed Sally out into the hall, sat down on a white leather chair and put on her shoes. Agatha drew a hundred-dollar bill out of her wallet. 'Meet me later?'

Sally knelt down at Agatha's feet. 'You got a speck on that there shoe. I'll just wipe it off.' And in a whisper, 'Jimmy's Bar down on Peach Tree. Eight o'clock.'

Agatha nodded. She went out to her waiting taxi and asked to be driven to the nearest hotel. 'There's a motel out on the freeway, not far,' said the driver. 'But you ain't got a car.'

'Give me your card and I'll phone you if I need you.' He passed over a grimy card.

'And where is Jimmy's Bar on Peach Tree.'

'That's just one block behind the motel.'

'Great.'

'Look, lady, if you goin' to need me tomorrow, you'd best fix a time, see. I cain't afford to sit around waiting for a fare.'

'Pick me up at nine in the morning.'

The motel was clean and efficient. Agatha unpacked a few belongings from her overnight case. She was feeling dizzy with jet lag. She turned her alarm clock back five hours to set it to American time. Then she telephoned Patrick.

'Don't tell anyone, Patrick, but I'm in America. Have you got any notes of the Courtney murder with you?'

'Got them somewhere here.'

'Tom Courtney's sister's alibi is someone called Harriet Temple. You didn't manage to get an address out of the police?'

'Can't remember. Hang on.'

Agatha waited impatiently. Outside on the freeway, the traffic swished past like some great mechanical ocean. At last Patrick came back on the phone. 'Got it. Harriet Temple ... got a pen?'

'Yes.'

'Divorcee. Address, Camden Court, apartment 5, number 252. Didn't get a phone number.'

'Thanks, Patrick. I'll tell you about it when I get back.'

Agatha showered and changed into a cool shirt dress and then went out to look for Jimmy's Bar.

As the driver had said, it was indeed only two blocks from the hotel, a red flashing light above the door proclaiming Jimmy's into the still, dark evening air.

Agatha opened the door and went in. There were a few men at the bar and some men and women seated in red imitation-leather booths along one wall.

She sat down in one of the booths that afforded a good look at the door. It was exactly eight o'clock.

Then Agatha realized there was no waiter service. She went up to the bar and ordered a bottle of Budweiser. 'May I have a glass, please?'

She braced herself for the usual sort of are-you-English questions but the barman looked too tired to waste time on starting a conversation. 'I'll be having a Bud as well,' said a voice at her elbow. Agatha turned and saw Sally. She paid for the drinks and led the way over to one of the booths.

'So what you want of me?' asked Sally.

'I thought you might have an idea if Mrs Courtney had any enemies.'

'Can't right say she could've had any. See, hardly anyone was allowed in the house, and that's a fact. Didn't like to take your money for nothin' but maybe you'd like to see these. Miz Bairns asked me to burn 'em and I clean forgot. Old family photos. Might help.'

Agatha took out her wallet and handed over a couple of hundred. She knew she probably didn't have to pay anything for them but there was a beaten-down weariness in Sally's brown face that went to her heart.

'Why do you stay in such a job?' asked Agatha.

'Pay's good. But with this money you just done give

me I'm off back home to Atlanta in the morning. I'd rather go back to waiting tables than work for her. Been there only three weeks. She follows me around like a cat. Looks for dirt. Crazy about dirt she is. She pays me end of the week, which is tomorrow. I'll collect that and then leave her a note. Now, I best get back.'

'Who worked for her before you?'

'Don't rightly know. I know she's only lived there a couple o' months.'

Agatha thanked her and wished her luck. She put the album in her briefcase. Now, she thought, as she headed back to the hotel, let's see why Amy was so keen to have this lot burned.

Agatha found to her surprise that there was a bowl of fruit and a bottle of sparkling wine on the bedside table. A note said, 'With compliments'.

Now that's nice, thought Agatha. How odd that such a functional type of roadside motel should go to such a courtesy.

She picked up the phone and got through to reception. 'I just want to thank you for the fruit and wine,' she said.

'We didn't give no fruit or wine to your room, ma'am. It's Mizz Raisin, isn't it?'

'Yes.'

'Maybe you got an admirer.'

Agatha slowly replaced the receiver. If by any chance the wine was drugged, she could pour some off, then pretend to be asleep and see if anyone came into the room.

On the other hand, that someone might kill her. She did not want to go to the police because it would take ages waiting for the contents of the wine bottle to be analysed, and the American police would contact Mircester, who would no doubt be furious at her interfering in their investigation.

She went downstairs to reception and said to the clerk 'I'm expecting a friend to arrive from England late tonight. May I book another room?'

'Sure, just fill out the form. There's one along the corridor from you. That do?'

'Fine.'

Agatha returned to her room and poured half the bottle of wine down the toilet after rinsing some of it around in a glass.

She made up the bed to look as if someone was asleep in it, finally placing a wig she kept for travelling stuffed with newspapers on the pillow. She opened the bedside drawer and took out a copy of the Gideon Bible and put it in her briefcase in the place of the photo album.

Then she went out, locking the door and letting herself into the extra room she had booked.

Agatha lay down on the bed and prepared to wait. But she was exhausted and jet-lagged and soon fell asleep, not waking until four in the morning.

She went out and walked slowly along to her old room. There wasn't any sign of forced entry. She unlocked the door and switched on the light. All seemed to be as she had left it but for one thing: the briefcase was gone. Gripped by panic, she packed up her few belongings, emptied out the wine in case one of the maids should drink it, went downstairs, paid her bills and phoned her taxi driver.

He grumbled a bit at being called out in the middle of the night but agreed to come.

When the cab arrived, she told the driver to take her to any large five-star hotel in the centre of the city.

He dropped her outside the Hilton Garden Inn. As Agatha stumbled wearily out of the cab, her handbag opened and the contents spilled on to the pavement. The driver helped her gather up the contents, including a packet of cigarettes. 'You won't be needing those,' he said.

'Why not?'

'Hotel's proud of the fact you can't do no smoking anywhere inside.'

'Oh, snakes and bastards,' howled Agatha. 'Take me somewhere where I can smoke.'

He drove her a few blocks to a boutique hotel called the Cloche. 'Wait there,' ordered Agatha. 'I want a look at this place first.'

The entrance hall was all mahogany and brass. Yes, said the night porter, he had a smoking room available. Agatha went out and paid off the taxi and then followed the porter, who was carrying her bag inside. The price was steep but the room she was ushered into was large and comfortable and boasted a small sitting room.

With a sigh of pleasure, she lit a cigarette, realizing she had not had one since leaving England. It tasted foul. Agatha studied the packet with narrowed eyes in case the cigarettes should turn out to be the contraband sweepings off some Chinese factory floor, but everything seemed correct. 'Rats!' she said to uncaring walls and went to bed instead, not waking until noon.

After showering and dressing, she ordered coffee and sandwiches and sat down to inspect the photograph album. She stared, puzzled, at various photographs. Someone appeared to have been cut out of quite a lot of them. There was Tom with his arm around someone who had been snipped out of the photograph; the same thing had been done to several of the others. There were a few of Miriam with her husbands on her wedding days.

'None of Amy,' said Agatha to the coffee pot. 'I wonder why.'

After she had finished her light lunch, she phoned her taxi driver. When she gave him the address of Camden Court, he looked puzzled. 'Don't you know it?' she asked impatiently.

'Sure, but you now being in this classy hotel and wanting to go to a place like Camden Court set me back a bit for a moment.'

'Why?'

'Bit out of town in the projects.'

'I've got to get there.'

'Okay, lady. You're the boss.'

Curious, very curious, thought Agatha. What is a frigid, rich queen like Amy doing with a pal in the projects? You'd think the very sight of a cockroach would make that sterile bitch faint.

The projects were not as insalubrious as Agatha had feared. She found number five and knocked at the door. The door was opened by a tall, tired-looking motherly woman with a bad perm and swollen ankles showing above scuffed slippers.

'Harriet Temple?' asked Agatha.

'I ain't buying.'

'And I'm not selling. I am a private inquiry agent working for Mr Tom Courtney.'

'Mr Courtney? You'd best come in.'

Agatha walked through to a cluttered living room. The furniture was shabby but there was an expensive flat-screen TV on one wall.

'I gather Mrs Bairns stayed with you at the time of her mother's murder?'

'That's right.'

'Are you an old friend of Mrs Bairns?'

'Used to be. My husband was a doctor but he lost his licence and was sent to prison for supplying drugs. Still Amy would visit from time to time. She bought me that TV there. Right generous.'

'This may seem odd but do you have any photographs of Mrs Bairns?'

Harriet laughed. 'Amy asked me that, too. I only had the few and I gave them to her. Mind you, I kept the one of my wedding 'cause she was my maid of honour. I didn't want to let go of that one.'

'May I see it?'

'I'll get it.'

She came back with a framed photo and handed it to Agatha. 'Where is Amy?' asked Agatha.

'Oh, of course she had all that cosmetic surgery. That's her.'

Agatha stared in amazement. Amy could almost have been her brother in drag. 'Are she and Tom twins?'

'Yes, identical. Mind you, it wasn't only her appearance that got changed. She just wasn't the same old Amy. Fussed about bugs and infections the whole time. Of course, she and Tom were always a bit like that.'

Agatha sat silently and then said slowly, 'Do you have a passport?'

'You know, Amy asked me that. I said I hadn't. So she said maybe she'd take me on a trip somewhere to make up for my man being in prison. Gave me that TV. She said if I gave her my birth certificate and everything, she'd fix it up for me. But I never heard no more about it. I went to see her – it must have been after she got all that cosmetic work and, I swear to God, I've never seen such a change in anyone.

'Didn't even ask me to sit down. Said she had her position in local society to think of, and having a friend whose husband was a criminal wouldn't do her any good. She asked me not to come back. I was so hurt I went home and cried my eyes out.'

Agatha took a small powerful camera out of her handbag. 'If I could just photograph that picture?'

'Well, I promised Amy I'd got rid of all of them . . . but what the hell? She isn't a friend any more. Go ahead.'

'You gave her an alibi for the time of her mother's murder. Did she really stay with you?'

'Of course,' said Harriet. 'I'm not a liar. Now, do you mind just getting out?'

A day later, Inspector Wilkes walked into Mircester police headquarters to be told by the desk sergeant that

Mrs Raisin was waiting to speak to him. Wilkes swung round. Fast asleep on a hard plastic chair was Agatha Raisin. Her mouth was open and she was snoring gently.

'Tell her I'm still out,' said Wilkes curtly.

'Sir, she said something about having solved the murder of Mrs Courtney.'

Wilkes scowled horribly. He hated to admit that Agatha had helped him in the past but he decided he'd better wake her up and hear what she had to say. He shook her by the shoulder. As Agatha blinked up at him, he demanded, 'What's all this about you having solved the murder?'

'Get me a strong black coffee and I'll tell you all about it,' said Agatha.

Fortunately for Agatha, Sergeant Collins was out on a job, so it was Bill Wong who sat with Wilkes as Agatha began her story. She described how Amy Courtney had changed her appearance drastically but that before that she had been a mirror image of her twin, Tom. Agatha theorized that it was Amy dressed as Tom who had gone to the Cayman Islands, that Harriet had been heavily bribed to say that Amy was staying with her, and that Amy had given Tom Harriet's birth certificate and all necessary details. Tom had made himself up as a woman and secured a passport in Harriet's name, flown to London and murdered his mother for her money.

'This is all very far-fetched,' said Wilkes.

'I bet you didn't check to see if someone called Harriet Temple had entered the country,' said Agatha.

'But why would this Harriet Temple continue to lie?'

'Check the airport and then ask her. If she thinks she's in danger of being accused of murder, she'll soon tell you. And I think Amy got all that cosmetic surgery in time for any police questions just in case someone should notice the likeness to her brother. But why should they? The murder was in England in a village where there is still an unsolved murder. She was just covering all the bases.'

'Well, keep away from Tom Courtney and that village until we check this out.'

Agatha called on Mrs Bloxby that evening to tell her the latest news. 'Do you really think they would go to such elaborate lengths?' asked the vicar's wife.

'Yes, I do. There's evidently a great deal of money involved. And what better place to commit a murder than in some small English village that already has had one?'

'You don't think that the murder of Sunday was to set the scene?' said Mrs Bloxby.

'No, I have a feeling that the murder of Grudge Sunday had nothing to do with the Courtney murder. Where is Tom Courtney? Does anyone know?'

'Yes, he called this morning looking for you. Said he was off to the States for a few days.'

'I'd better tell Wilkes. If he is guilty, he might make a run for it and Harriet Temple may need protection.'

'Use our phone.'

'I thought your phone was the sole property of your husband.'

'Oh, Alf won't mind.'

Mrs Bloxby went off to her husband's study. Agatha grinned as she could hear the vicar's voice raised in anger. 'This is not a detective agency and yet you involve yourself with that woman and her folly.'

Agatha took out her own phone and dialled Wilkes. She was told curtly that he was too busy to speak to her.

'Sod them all,' said Agatha. 'I'm taking my jet lag home to bed.'

The first thing she saw when she drove up outside her cottage was the crumpled figure of Toni Gilmour sitting on her doorstep.

Agatha hurried out of her car. 'Toni, my dear. What is the matter?'

'It's Sharon. She's disappeared.'

'Oh, no! Come in.'

'Where have you been?' wailed Toni.

'I've been in the States. Come through to the kitchen and tell me about Sharon.'

'She came round to my flat a few days ago and said you'd fired her and she wanted a place to stay. Honestly, I couldn't bear the thought of her mess again so I said she'd best go. She burst into tears. Why did you fire her?'

'I accused her of being on drugs. She told me to sod the job and a few choice insults and stormed off.'

'I've gone looking for her round the clubs,' said Toni. 'She's been hanging around with a lot of bikers. They're bad news. There's one in particular, Jazz Belter, and he's ancient!'

'How ancient?'

'In his forties.'

Agatha winced.

'With a balding head and a ponytail. Real stereotype. I think he's the one who's been supplying her with drugs. They hang out at the Shamrock pub out on the bypass.'

'Toni, I'll give Sharon her job back again but she's got to get herself cleaned up.'

'But I can't find her!'

'Have you told the police?'

'Not yet.'

'Make some coffee, will you? I'll phone them right away. Wait a minute! Surely her parents have reported her missing?'

'No, she told them she was living with me.'

'I'll call Bill.'

Bill was at the station and listened to Agatha's story about the missing Sharon.

'She's been found,' said Bill in a quiet voice.

'Oh, that's great. Poor Toni's been going out of her mind with—'

'Agatha! Listen! Sharon's dead.'

'How? When?'

'She was found a few hours ago. She had been stabbed and strung up on a lamppost on a back street. Her mouth was stuffed with grass. I know some of the bikers, went to school with a few. Said Sharon had been drinking and drugging and bragging how she was really working undercover. Her boyfriend, Jazz Belter, had just dumped her and it's thought she was trying to scare him.'

'Who did it?'

'We're looking for Jazz at the moment.'

'I'll be with you as soon as I can.'

'You can't do anything. Get a good night's sleep.'

Toni looked at Agatha white-faced as Agatha slowly replaced the receiver.

Agatha told her the story. Toni began to cry, dismal wracking sobs shaking her whole body.

Agatha flapped hopelessly around her, wondering what to do. I should hug her or something, she thought. Then she went through to the sitting room and called Mrs Bloxby, who said she would be round immediately.

Agatha walked up and down the garden fifteen minutes later, smoking furiously, while Mrs Bloxby, the expert comforter, got to work. Agatha could hear the vicar's wife's soothing voice through the open kitchen door.

'Of course her death has nothing to do with you, Toni. It wasn't your fault that she started taking drugs and got into bad company. Everyone feels guilty when someone close to them dies, wondering this way and that if they could have done anything. Now, dry your eyes. No, don't drink coffee. Drink this hot sweet tea. So much better for shock. You gather up your things. You're coming home with me for the night.'

Agatha would have gone with them, but Mrs Bloxby stopped her with a little warning shake of the head.

Doris Simpson was still looking after Agatha's cats. 'I wish I had someone to look after me,' said Agatha.

'My shoulders aren't very broad,' said a familiar voice. 'But you could try and lean.'

'Charles!' Agatha burst into tears.

'Good heavens! What's happened to old iron-knickers Raisin? Come on, girl, up on your feet! We'll move into the sitting room, get ourselves a drink and you can tell me all about it.'

Charles listened while Agatha talked on and on about Sharon's death and then about her trip to Philadelphia. 'You did well,' he said when she had finished talking. 'I thought Courtney was weird. As for Sharon? Well, that was always going to be a disaster, but you couldn't seem to see it.'

'Why didn't you say something?'

'Would you have listened?'

'Perhaps not.'

'Did you tell her to go undercover and find out about these bikers?'

'No.'

'Well, there you are. It's a damned shame. There's nothing we can do tonight. Let's get some sleep. I'll just get my bag out of the car.'

But when Charles returned, Agatha was fast asleep. He lifted her legs up and stretched her out on the sofa, went upstairs and came back with a duvet to cover her, and then took himself off to bed in the spare room.

Agatha was awakened early the next morning by the shrilling of the doorbell. She struggled up from the sofa and went to answer it.

A policewoman stood there. 'Mrs Raisin, I'm to take you to headquarters to go over your statement.'

'Give me a few minutes to wash and change,' groaned Agatha. 'Don't you want to come in?'

'I'll wait in the car.'

Agatha had a quick shower and change of clothes. Then she went into the spare room where Charles lay peacefully sleeping. She shook him awake. 'I've got to go to headquarters. Are you coming?'

He yawned and turned on his side. 'You'll do fine all by yourself.'

'Story of my life,' muttered Agatha, stomping down the stairs.

Chapter Six

Agatha learned that the American police were currently hunting for both Tom Courtney and his sister. Tom had left the UK the day after Agatha had taken her flight to the States. Harriet Temple had cracked and said that Amy had initially told her she needed an excuse because she was having an affair. After the murder, when Harriet read about it and phoned her, Amy had threatened to kill her if she ever breathed a word. Dr Bairns was crying and bewildered, saying he did not know where his wife was. The Courtneys had cleared out their bank accounts and disappeared.

Agatha thought they must have moved very fast indeed. It seemed likely that Tom had fled just after Amy had telephoned him to report Agatha's visit.

'So when we get them and have them extradited, Courtney will be charged with the murder of his mother and also of John Sunday.'

'But why on earth would he kill John Sunday?'

'He knew where his mother lived. The killing of Sunday was just setting the scene.'

'But is there any record of him entering the country at that time?'

'No, but we're working on it. He may have played the same trick on someone that his sister played on Harriet and got another passport. He was setting the stage. It turns out that both he and his sister have at various times been hospitalized for drugs and depression. There are psychiatric reports claiming they both suffered from a form of narcissistic psychopathy. They were the children of Mrs Courtney's first marriage. He thought with one murder already in that village, we wouldn't look at him.'

'Why employ me?'

'Because he felt perfectly sure you wouldn't find anything. He told Bill Wong that perhaps he had made a mistake employing what he called "a mere village sleuth" but that he was willing to try anything.'

'I don't think the murder of John Sunday had anything to do with it,' said Agatha. 'It's just one elaborate step too far.'

'So you say. But as far as we're concerned, that murder is solved. The American police will get a confession out of him.'

'If they ever catch him,' said Agatha cynically. 'At the moment, I'm going all out to get the bastard who killed Sharon.'

'You needn't bother. It was Jazz Belter. Real name Fred Belter. We've got him in the cells.'

'How did you get him so quickly?'

'Detective Wong interviewed an old lady who lived in the flats overlooking where the dead girl was found. She doesn't sleep much. She saw Belter drag Sharon out of the boot of a car, stuff her mouth with grass, sling a rope over the lamppost – it's one of those old-fashioned kind – and string her up. He was so high on drugs when we picked him up, it took four officers to hold him down and handcuff him.'

Agatha left police headquarters feeling very low. Somehow, if finding out the murderer of poor Sharon had turned out to be a complicated affair, it might have made the girl's death seem less useless, less of such a complete waste of a young life.

She had a sudden vivid memory of looking down from the office window and watching Sharon and Toni going off for the evening, laughing and with their arms around each other.

She went round to the office. Patrick and Toni were out on jobs. Mrs Freedman had gone off to do some shopping and Phil Marshall was manning the phones. Phil was in his seventies, a quiet man with a shock of white hair. He had retained a good figure. He was an expert cameraman.

'Bad business about Sharon,' said Phil. 'Mrs Freedman won't be long. Do you want me to give you a rundown on what we are all doing?'

'Not at the moment. I need to get back to thinking about the murder of John Sunday to take my mind off Sharon's death.'

'So you don't think the Courtneys did it?'

'No. It's nagging at the back of my mind that it was someone in that village. You see the trouble with being a town person and not a village person and meeting so many other incomers these days,' said Agatha. 'I can't help feeling that people like me don't really know village life, what really goes on in the minds of the genuine villagers. It's not even like some of those television series you see based on supposed village life. All so politically correct. If the local retired major was in the army, then he's either a fascist or a closet gay. Gypsies are always good people and not understood. I saw one with eight murders and not a pressman in sight.

'No. I suspect there are undercurrents in an off-the-tourist-map sort of place like Odley Cruesis. Unless it was someone at John's work ... Oh, Mrs Freedman, you're back. Would you please look me out the files on John Sunday?'

'No need for that,' said Phil. 'I've got it all on the computer.'

Agatha fetched herself a strong cup of coffee and lit a cigarette. Mrs Freedman stifled a sigh and opened a window. Agatha sat down in front of the computer and began to read all the reports along with Phil's photographs. Then she said, 'Something's missing.'

'What?' asked Phil.

'Where did John Sunday live?'

'I remember that. A terraced house. Oxford Lane in Mircester. Patrick said the police could not find anything that related to the murder.'

'And who got the house?'

'Wait and I'll get my notebook.'

'Phil, it should be in here with the rest.'

Agatha bit her lip in vexation. What with the murder of Miriam and then her own hip-replacement operation, she felt she had often too easily assumed that both murders were connected.

'Let me see.' Phil came back with a notebook and flicked the pages. 'Ah, here we are. I went with Patrick. Number seven, Oxford Lane. Two up, two down terraced house. Small front garden. Neighbourhood slightly run down. He was never married. His sister inherited. A Mrs Parker. Probably sold the house.'

'Maybe not. I'd love a look inside, just in case there's anything left. Let's drive round there.'

The house had a small, weedy front garden. As Agatha pushed open the front gate, a neighbour opened her door and called out, 'Are you the house clearance people?'

'Yes,' said Agatha on the spur of the moment.

'Wait and I'll get the key,' said the neighbour. 'Mrs Parker's still up north but she'll be here tomorrow. She's been right poorly and hasn't been able to get round to doing anything about her brother's house before this. She got in touch with you lot to sell off everything. She and her brother had a quarrel a long time ago and she didn't want to have anything to do with his stuff. She came down after his murder – poor man – and took away a few things, but she didn't want the rest.'

'We shouldn't be doing this,' muttered Phil.

'Shh! This is a great opportunity.'

When the neighbour came back with the key, Agatha said, 'I'm surprised Mrs Parker took so long to call us in and put the house up for sale.'

'Well, like I said, she's poorly and she couldn't find the time before. Let me have the key when you've finished.'

Once inside, Phil said angrily, 'And what do we do if the real people turn up?'

'We'll leave the front door open,' said Agatha. 'If we hear them arriving, we'll just nip out the back way.'

The downstairs consisted of a living room and kitchen on one side of the dark passage and a study on the other. Upstairs were two bedrooms and one bathroom.

'I suppose the study's the place to start,' said Agatha, 'although the police are sure to be still hanging on to all his paperwork until his sister claims it.'

'I'll try the other rooms,' said Phil. 'Have you considered, Agatha, that when the real clearance people turn up, that neighbour is going to report us to the police and give our descriptions?'

'She seemed to be very shortsighted,' said Agatha hopefully.

Phil went off and Agatha began to search diligently, but it all too soon appeared that the police had taken away every bit of paper they could get their hands on. She took out the desk drawers in case anything was taped to the undersides, but there was nothing, except on the bottom of one drawer was 'A119X' written in felt-tipped pen. Agatha wrote it down.

They spent over an hour searching for secret hiding places but finding none. It was bleakly furnished with the bare essentials. It seemed as if John Sunday had liked puzzles and jigsaws. One of the few human touches in the living room was a bookshelf containing boxes of jigsaw puzzles and crossword books. There were no photographs. A mirror hung over the fireplace reflecting the gloomy room. Phil thought that maybe the houses

111

had been built for workers because the terrace faced north and didn't get much sunlight and he had noticed the building bricks were of poor quality.

They even searched under the cushions of the shabby brown corduroy sofa and down the sides of two armchairs. Phil reported that only one of the upstairs bedrooms had been used and that the other was completely empty.

When they left and locked up, Agatha had an idea. She took the key back to the neighbour and, reverting to the Birmingham accent of her youth, she said, 'Made an awful mistake, love. Should've been round the corner in Oxford Terrace. Please don't tell Mrs Parker or we'll get in awful trouble.'

The neighbour peered at her. 'Don't you be worrying yourself, m'dear. We all get like that when we get older. Didn't I put the kettle on yesterday and clean forgot till it nearly burned dry?'

'That woman can hardly see a thing,' muttered Agatha crossly to Phil. 'I'm hungry. I need something to eat.'

They decided on a pub lunch at the George in Mircester. 'I wish I knew what A119X stood for,' said Agatha, 'and why it was written on the underside of the drawer. He liked puzzles. Nasty, devious mind, he probably had. He was probably the sort who would go to endless lengths to hide something somewhere difficult instead of just renting a safe deposit box.'

'Library!' said Phil suddenly.

'What library?' asked Agatha.

'I mean A119X looks like a number on the back of one of the Mircester Public Library books. They send a mobile library van round the villages and I borrow books from them. The library still uses the old card system.'

At the library, by asking at the desk, they discovered that A119X was a book entitled *Go to the Ant* by Percival Bright-Simmel. 'I'm afraid it hasn't been returned,' said the librarian. 'We meant to send out the usual letter reminding the borrower that the book was overdue but when we found out it was that John Sunday who was murdered, well, we just needed to give it up for lost. We would have got rid of it pretty soon as we're due for an overhaul. No one else had taken that book out for a long time.'

'What kind of book was it?' asked Phil.

'It was in the non-fiction religious section.'

Outside the library, Agatha said, 'We've got to get back into Sunday's house and search the bookshelves. What was so important about that book?'

But when they arrived back at Sunday's house, it was to find a van outside the door bearing the legend 'Pyrson's House Clearance'. The door was standing open. Agatha looked cautiously towards the house next door but there was no sign of the neighbour who had given them the key.

'What are you doing?' hissed Phil as Agatha strode up towards the open door.

'I know what I'm doing,' said Agatha. She walked inside. Two men were crating up furniture.

'I'm from Mircester Library,' said Agatha. 'The previous owner failed to return one of our books. Do you mind if I take a quick look for it?'

'Go ahead,' said one of the men. 'We ain't got around to them yet.'

Phil had tentatively followed Agatha in. They both began to search the bookshelves. 'Puzzles and more puzzles,' muttered Agatha. 'Maybe there's something behind the books.' She began to pull them out. Phil was standing on a chair searching the top shelves when he said, 'Got something here. Yes, this is it. It was down behind the others along with this.'

'This' was a full bottle of whisky. 'Hey!' shouted one of the removal men. 'That there bottle's part o' the house contents.'

'You're welcome to it,' said Agatha. 'All we want is the book.'

They handed over the bottle of whisky and, clutching the book, made their way out of the house.

'What if that neighbour sees us?' fretted Phil. 'You told her we should have been round the corner at another house.'

'Oh, she'll just think we're part of the same business,' said Agatha airily. 'Let's get back to the office and have a good look, although it's not much of a book.' *Go to the Ant* was a thin, shabby book with an illustration on the front of a blond and blue-eyed Jesus Christ pointing accusingly, rather in the manner of the First World War posters that said 'Your Country Needs You'.

114

Toni was sitting at her computer typing up notes when they went into the office. Agatha noticed that the girl looked pale and listless. Must hire another young person, she thought. Maybe that will cheer her up. Agatha knew that the murder of Sharon had hit Toni hard.

'Stop typing, Toni,' she said, 'and help us with this.' She told Toni about how and why they had found the book.

The book turned out to be a sort of extended religious tract, written in 1926. It was a series of moral tales about unfortunate people who had behaved like the grass-hopper and ended up starving to death or living in the workhouse.

'You wouldn't think he was a religious sort of person,' said Phil. 'I mean, he made trouble for two churches that we know of. There are no clues here. No words underlined.'

'Let me see.' Toni took the thin book and began to riffle through the pages. 'I think I've got something.' She ran her hand lightly over one of the pages. 'There are some pin pricks under some letters.'

'Good girl!' Agatha seized a pen. 'Read them out.'

'This page has a u and then an n. Nothing next page. Wait a bit. Other page a d and an e.' She steadily worked her way through the book until she had one whole message. It read, 'Under the garden shed'.

'I'd better get back there tonight,' said Agatha. 'But why a secret message to himself? If he buried something under the garden shed, then why bother to go through this elaborate business? Are you game for another visit, Phil?'

Toni saw the reluctant look on Phil's face and said, 'I'll come with you.'

'Go and get some rest,' said Agatha. 'I'll call for you around midnight.'

When she got back to her cottage, there was no sign of Charles. She felt suddenly bereft. Surely she should be used to him dropping in and out of her life? She petted her faithless cats who wriggled away from her and stood by the garden door waiting to be let out.

She microwaved herself a dish of lasagne and moodily ate it at the kitchen table. Agatha decided to put an advertisement in the papers for a trainee detective. If Toni had a young person to train, it might take her mind off Sharon. What if, she wondered guiltily, I hadn't told Sharon to leave Toni's flat? Would she still be alive? No, she decided, she might even have started to bring the bikers to Toni's place and there might have been two dead bodies instead of one.

Agatha changed into dark clothes, set the alarm for eleven-thirty and lay down on the sofa. As she drifted off to sleep, she wondered why she had never put a cat flap in the garden door.

Agatha parked her car round the corner from where John Sunday's house lay and she and Toni made their way quietly along the deserted street. A thin drizzle was falling, and water was beginning to drip down from the trees that lined the street.

They opened the gate quietly and made their way along a brick path at the side of the house, which led to the back garden. Agatha risked flicking the thin beam of light from a pencil torch round the small area of garden. There was an unkempt lawn, several laurel bushes and the black silhouette of a small shed in the far right-hand corner.

Agatha flicked her torch on again and shone it on the door. 'There's a padlock,' whispered Toni.

'I thought there might be,' said Agatha, opening up a carrier bag and hauling out a pair of bolt cutters. 'Soon get this open.'

'But what if the sister finds the broken padlock and reports the shed has been broken into?'

'I brought another padlock,' said Agatha cheerfully. 'No one will know the difference.'

She cut through the padlock and opened the door. The shed had a wooden floor. Agatha handed Toni the torch and said, 'Your eyes are better than mine. Crouch down there and see if you can find any marks where something might have been hidden. We don't want to smash up the whole floor.'

Toni crawled around and then shook her head. 'Nothing.'

'I was afraid of that,' said Agatha gloomily. 'We're going to have to try and lift all the planks up.'

'Wait a bit.' Toni sat back on her knees. 'This shed is raised up a bit from the ground. What if all we have to do is go outside and have a look underneath?'

'Great! Let's try it. I'll put this new padlock on just in

case anyone comes after us and we have to make a quick getaway.'

Toni lay down on the wet grass and shone the torch under the shed. 'There's something here,' she said.

A voice sounded from next door. 'I assure you, officer, I heard voices coming from Mr Sunday's garden.'

'Snakes and bastards,' muttered Agatha. 'Grab whatever it is and we'll run.'

Toni pulled out a small metal box. They ran to the end of the small garden, Toni vaulted over the gate clutching the box, Agatha threw her carrier bag over and heaved herself over the wooden gate and fell in a heap in the lane outside.

'Quietly,' hissed Toni, feeling that Agatha charging off down the lane was making as much noise as a stampeding elephant.

With relief, they reached the safety of Agatha's car and drove off.

Once back at the cottage, Toni put the metal box on the kitchen table. 'It's locked,' she said. 'Now, what do we do?'

Agatha opened a kitchen drawer by the sink and took out a chisel. She also handed Toni a thin pair of latex gloves and put a pair on herself. She wedged the end in the slit by the lock and prised down hard. There was a loud snap and the lid flew back.

There was a package wrapped in tough white plastic. Agatha took the kitchen scissors and cut it open. There were photographs and letters. 'Look at this!' exclaimed

Agatha. 'That's a naked Tilly Glossop on top of some man, but who's the man?'

'It's hard to see his face, all contorted like it is. But it looks suspiciously like the mayor of Cirencester. I'll look him up on your computer and get a photograph.'

'You go ahead. I'll look at these others. Oh, my!'

Toni paused in the doorway. 'Oh, what?'

'It's a photo of Penelope Timson necking passionately with some fellow who isn't the vicar. The dirty little man must have been blackmailing people.' As Toni went through to the computer, Agatha studied the few letters. They were passionate love letters from people she did not know and written to people she did not know either.

She lit a cigarette and wondered what to do. Toni came back in. 'Yes, it's the mayor all right. Shall we go and confront him tomorrow?'

'No,' said Agatha. 'He'll call his lawyer. The police will be called in. Where did we get this? Why were we withholding evidence? Penelope Timson is a friend of Mrs Bloxby. I'll keep that photo back. We'll wipe everything we've touched carefully and send the package to the police. No, that won't do. They've got to find it themselves. Damn, we've got to put it back.'

'What about the broken lock?'

'I've got a metal box just like it. I used to keep jewellery in it until I got a proper jewel case. I'll get it, we'll pop the stuff in and back under the shed it goes.'

'And how do the police find it?'

'I'll call them from a phone box. I've got this nifty little machine. It's a portable voice distorter.'

* * *

119

This time they were able to enter and exit the garden without being heard. Agatha made the phone call to police headquarters and then they drove to an all-night restaurant out on the motorway for an early breakfast.

After a breakfast of sausage, bacon, egg and chips and two cups of black coffee, Agatha said, 'First, we should both get some sleep. I think I'll talk to Mrs Bloxby about Penelope and suggest we both approach her. Now, the big question is Tilly Glossop. She and Sunday may have been blackmailing the mayor together. I mean, someone had to be on hand to take that photograph.'

'Do you want me to try Tilly?'

'I think maybe Patrick might be a better idea. He still looks like a cop and he might frighten her into some sort of confession or slip-up.'

Agatha snatched a few hours' sleep and turned up in the office at nine the next morning to brief Patrick. Then she told Mrs Freedman to put in an advertisement for another detective. 'A trainee, mind,' cautioned Agatha. 'Some student in his or her gap year would do. I'm off to see Mrs Bloxby about something. Seems a quiet morning. Want to come, Toni?'

Toni agreed. She still mourned her lost friend, Sharon, and felt the vicarage and Mrs Bloxby's quiet presence would be very soothing.

Despite the loud protests from the study from the vicar, shouting, 'This place is getting like Piccadilly Circus!'

Mrs Bloxby settled them in the vicarage drawing room. Rain was falling steadily outside. 'They said it was going to be a barbecue summer,' said Agatha. 'Such a shame for all the families who booked their holidays in Britain this year.'

'Amazing thing, British tourism,' remarked Mrs Bloxby when she returned from the kitchen with a laden tray. 'People flit by air to countries and never really understand other races or cultures, like dragonflies flitting over a pond. Can't see the murky depth underneath. You are looking unusually serious, Mrs Raisin.'

Agatha opened her capacious handbag and drew out a white envelope and handed it to the vicar's wife. 'Before you look at that, I'll tell you how we came by it.'

She described how they had found the box under Sunday's shed. 'I extracted the one photo in that envelope, which is withholding evidence from the police, but I wanted to consult you first.'

Mrs Bloxby took out the photo and slowly sat down. 'Oh, dear. What shall we do?'

'I thought as you knew her, we might go over there and have a quiet word. I cannot for a moment think that Mrs Timson was ever involved with anyone capable of murder. If you think for one moment she might have got involved with some sort of villain, I can post this anonymously to the police.'

'Have some tea and scones,' urged Mrs Bloxby. 'Tea and scones are very mind settling.'

'Have you ever heard any gossip about Mrs Timson?' asked Toni.

'Nothing at all,' said Mrs Bloxby. 'Oh, dear, perhaps it

might have been better if you had both left the matter to the police. They would probably send along a policewoman and . . .'

'They would probably send along Detective Sergeant Collins, who would frighten her to death and no doubt lead her off in handcuffs in front of the whole village,' said Agatha harshly.

Mrs Bloxby sighed. 'I might as well go with you. Dear me, what sinks of iniquity these little villages can be.'

The rain had stopped as they drove in Agatha's car to Odley Cruesis. Sunlight gilded the puddles of water on the road and glittering raindrops plopped from the branches of the overhead trees. As they climbed out of the car in front of the vicarage, the air smelled sweet and fresh.

Penelope answered the door and smiled when she saw them. 'Please come in. My husband is over at the church.'

'Good,' said Agatha, 'It's you we want to see.'

'Come through. Coffee?'

'No, we've just had some,' said Agatha. She opened her handbag, took out the envelope and extracted the photograph, which she handed to Penelope. Penelope sank down on to a corner of the sofa and hunched herself up and wrapped her arms around her thin body. Mrs Bloxby sat beside her and put a comforting arm around her shoulders. 'Mrs Timson, Mrs Raisin has taken a great risk in not showing this photo to the police. Was Mr Sunday blackmailing you?'

Penelope gulped and burst into tears. Toni fetched a box of tissues from a side table and handed it to her. Agatha waited impatiently, hoping the vicar would not walk in on the scene. At last Penelope gave a shuddering sigh. 'Yes, he was.'

'Who was the man?' asked Agatha.

'He was a visiting American preacher. Giles asked me to show him around the Cotswolds. We became friendly. He was a widower. He told a lot of very funny jokes. Giles never tells jokes. Jokes can be very seductive,' she said plaintively.

'So you had an affair!'

'Oh, no!' Penelope looked shocked. 'It was the morning before he left. We were in the churchyard and he thanked me for taking care of him and he swept me into his arms and kissed me. Then he laughed and said, "I shouldn't have done that." I said, "No, you shouldn't," and he patted me on the shoulder and went in to say goodbye to Giles.'

'And did Sunday start to blackmail you?'

'Not exactly. He came round one morning three days later when Giles was over in a neighbouring parish and showed me the photograph. I explained it was just a kiss, but he said my husband would never believe that if he saw the photograph. I asked him what he wanted. He laughed nastily and said he'd get back to me.'

'And when was this?' asked Mrs Bloxby.

'Three days before he was murdered,' whispered Penelope. 'He phoned me the day before the protest meeting and said I had to get it stopped or he would send the photo to Giles. I couldn't bear it any longer.

They always say that blackmailers never go away. So I told Giles.'

Mrs Bloxby said sympathetically, 'Giles must have been furious.'

'It was worse than that,' said Penelope. 'He laughed and laughed. "Forget it," he said. "I mean, just look in the mirror. Everyone knows Americans are over affectionate. I'll go and see Sunday and we'll never hear another word."

'After the murder, I asked him if he had said anything to the police or if he had gone to see Sunday, and he said he hadn't had the time to see Sunday and he had no intention of mentioning the silly photo to the police.'

What have I done now? wondered Agatha miserably. I should have left the photo for the police to find. I believe Penelope. But they would have grilled Giles and checked on his movements. He wasn't with the party when John was stabbed.

'We'll leave it for the moment,' said Agatha.

When they left the vicarage, Mrs Bloxby said, 'Let's go somewhere quiet. I'm beginning to remember things.'

'My kitchen is the quietest place around here,' said Agatha, setting off in the direction of home.

Once seated in Agatha's kitchen, Mrs Bloxby began. 'I remember it was last autumn and I remember the visiting preacher. His name was Silas Cuttler. American from some Episcopal church somewhere. He was a round,

124

jolly man. Around that time, Mrs Timson smartened her appearance and even wore make-up.'

'Is Penelope Timson verbally abused?' asked Agatha.

'Oh, just the usual married stuff. "What's that muck on your face? You are silly." Usual things like that. Giles is rather a cold, impatient sort of man.'

'I think I ought to ask him some questions,' said Agatha.

'My dear Mrs Raisin, he would coldly accuse you of withholding police evidence, take it to the police himself and then you would really be in trouble. I am sure Mr Timson can't for one moment think his wife is capable of having an adulterous affair.'

'And I can't interview the mayor because the police would wonder how I got on to him. Perhaps I'll just leave it for a few days and then get Patrick to find out from his police contacts what's been happening.'

Agatha asked Toni if she would like to go through the applications for the job of trainee detective and pick out a few suitable candidates, but Toni was still mourning the loss of her friend and so Agatha took a bundle of letters home one evening.

The advertisement had said that applicants must include copies of school certificates and a photograph.

Patrick called at her cottage and followed her through to the kitchen, where letters and photographs were spread across the kitchen table. 'I'm looking for a trainee,' said Agatha. 'But they seem to be a hopeless lot. What brings you?'

'Good news. Tom Courtney has been arrested outside Washington and has been charged with the murder of his mother. He was living with a woman in Mount Vernon and she turned him in to the police. She didn't know he was wanted for murder. She became afraid when he started scrubbing out all her closets and shelves and making her take a shower about five times a day. She asked him to leave and when he wouldn't, she called the police. They thought it was just a domestic, but some sharp-eyed trooper recognized Tom from a photo pinned up in the precinct.'

'When are they going to extradite him?'

'It'll take ages, if ever.'

'At least I don't need to be afraid of him turning up here. What about sister Amy?'

'Nothing, and he swears blind he doesn't know where she is. Husband hasn't heard from her. Complains she emptied their joint bank account before she cleared off. Anyway, Tom Courtney says he had nothing to do with the death of Sunday. Of course, at first the police here wanted that tied up, so they didn't believe him. But when I heard from my contacts that they found letters and a naughty photo of the mayor under the shed in his garden, they wearily decided to open the investigation again. Tilly Glossop and the mayor say it was a one-night fling after a boozy party at the town hall and that they weren't being blackmailed. The e-mails he seems to have stolen out of people's computers at the office. He used them for power, not money. Seems to be why he kept his job when there were so many complaints against him.'

'Sit down, Patrick. A cold beer?'

'Great. I'm driving but one wouldn't hurt.'

Although retired from the force, Patrick always looked somehow like a policeman, with his neatly cropped brown hair, lugubrious face, well-pressed clothes and shiny black shoes.

'Apart from Tilly Glossop, no one else is connected to Odley Cruesis,' said Patrick. 'Tilly is still in for questioning and has had to surrender her passport.'

Agatha thought guiltily of the evidence she had suppressed.

She handed Patrick a glass of beer and then sat down at the table beside him and lit a cigarette. 'Look at these applications,' she said, sending a haze of cigarette smoke over the table. 'Most of them don't even seem able to write and a lot of them use text messaging language.'

'There's one fallen under the table,' said Patrick, bending down to retrieve it. 'Oh, look at this. Do you think he escaped from a production of *Il Pagliacci*?'

'Pally who?' demanded Agatha crossly, suspecting a dreaded intellectual reference that would show the gaping holes in her knowledge of the arts.

'The clown in opera. The one who sings "On With the Motley".'

'Let me see.'

Patrick handed her a photograph. It was a head-and-shoulders picture of a teenager. He had a mop of thick curly black hair, large hooded eyes, a prominent curved beak of a nose and a long mobile mouth. 'Four A-levels,' said Patrick. 'Doesn't want to be landed with a university loan and would like to find work right away.

Says he's intuitive, hardworking and gets on with people. Eighteen years old.'

'I'll have him in for an interview,' said Agatha. 'Toni needs someone young to cheer her up.'

'What's his name?'

'Simon Black.'

Simon entered Agatha's office at seven o'clock the following evening. He turned out to be quite small, perhaps just about five feet and two inches. He was very slim and slight so that his head looked disproportionately large. His eyes under their hooded lids were very large and black and glittered with a combination of humour and intelligence. Agatha thought that he looked like something that had escaped from *Lord of the Rings*.

'Tell me about yourself,' said Agatha.

'I think you'll find it's all in my CV.'

'Look, dear boy, if you want this job, try to sell yourself.'

'May I sit down?'

'Do.'

Simon pulled forward a chair and sat facing Agatha. He was dressed in black: black T-shirt, black trousers, socks and shoes. 'I'm clever about people,' said Simon. He had a slight Gloucestershire accent. 'I instinctively know when people are lying. I am above average intelligence and—'

'And you've got a very high opinion of yourself,' snapped Agatha.

'So you find listening to me selling myself offensive?'

asked Simon. He sounded as if he genuinely wanted to know.

Agatha gave a reluctant smile. 'I've had a bad day. Do you live with your parents?'

'No, I live by myself. My parents are dead. They died last year in a car crash. I wasn't left much but debts, even after the house was sold, so I decided it would be better to go out to work than have the burden of a university loan hanging over me. I've had enough of debts.'

The door of the office opened and Toni came in. 'I left something in my desk,' she said.

Agatha felt a pang as she looked at Toni's sad face. She had a sudden idea. 'Toni, this is Simon Black, who will be starting work with us tomorrow. Simon, Toni Gilmour. Are you busy at the moment, Toni?'

'Well . . . no.'

'Get some money from the petty cash and take Simon for a drink and introduce him to the world of detecting. You can charge for the overtime.'

'All right,' said Toni listlessly.

'Simon, report to this office at nine o'clock tomorrow and our secretary will give you a contract to sign.'

'Thank you ver—' began Simon but Agatha waved a dismissive hand. 'Off you both go.'

Agatha waited until they had gone down the stairs and out into the street. She rose and crossed to the window. They were walking along, several feet apart, not talking.

Chapter Seven

In the George pub next to police headquarters, Simon ordered a beer and Toni a half of lager.

'Which school did you go to?' asked Toni.

'Mircester Grammar.'

'I could have gone there myself,' said Toni, 'but my mother said she couldn't afford the uniform.'

'A lot of the kids can't. That's why they have a secondhand clothes store in the school.'

'Well, my mum was having a bit of difficulty then,' said Toni. 'Let's talk about the job. What do you want to know?'

'I want to know first of all if Agatha Raisin is a good boss. You look downtrodden and miserable.'

'I lost a friend I used to work with.'

'That girl, Sharon, who was murdered?'

Toni nodded.

'Is the job that dangerous?'

'No. Not often. It's usually routine stuff – missing pets and children, unfaithful wives and husbands. Sharon got into bad company. Bikers.'

'Have you been to grief or bereavement counselling?'

'Nothing like that. I wasn't family. She was just a

friend and a friend I was well and truly fed up with just before she died.'

'Have you been to Pyrt Park?'

Toni looked at him in surprise. 'No, why?'

'They've got a truly evil roller coaster. Drink up. That's where we're going.'

'Why on earth . . . ?'

'You'll see.'

He had a motorbike parked in the square. He handed Toni a helmet and put on his own.

'This is mad,' said Toni when they got to the entrance to the amusement park.

'Trust me.'

'I've never been on a roller coaster before. I might get sick.'

'You won't. Follow me.'

When they were strapped in, their chair began to move up and up and up until Toni could see the Malvern Hills in the distance. As they reached the crest, she clutched Simon's arm. 'I don't think I can take this.' The car plunged down and Toni screamed and screamed. She screamed like a banshee through the whole ride and when Simon helped her out at the end, she felt her legs wobble.

'What was that all about?' she asked weakly.

'It's scream therapy. I came here when my parents were killed. Don't worry about the job, I'll pick it up as I go along. Oh, look, candy floss! I'll get us some.'

131

He danced off, turning round to grin at her. What an odd boy, thought Toni. Like a jester. All he needs is a cap and bells.

But that night, she slept as she had not slept since the news of Sharon's murder.

In the morning, Simon signed his contract. He blinked in surprise at the generosity of his pay and looked across at Agatha. 'I'm taking you on full-time. I have a hunch about you,' said Agatha. 'Mind you, you are still on trial. Now, I was going to start you on some of the small stuff but I need a new pair of eyes. Do you remember reading about the murder of John Sunday?'

'Yes.'

'I want you to read up everything on it. Work all day on it and see if you can come up with any ideas. You'll find it all on the computer at that desk over there.'

Agatha caught a bleak look from Toni and thought with irritation, yes, I know it was Sharon's desk but I can hardly lay a wreath on it and burn candles. Agatha introduced him to the staff.

Simon sat down and got to work. He could dimly hear Agatha discussing other assignments. He concentrated on the files on the computer, shutting everything else out, including thoughts about Toni. He had been in love, once disastrously, and he never wanted to suffer hurt like that again. Toni, with her fair good looks, intelligence and disarming air of innocence, was danger.

As he read the reports, he tried to conjure up the scene in the vicarage drawing room when the dying Sunday

132

had appeared at the window. Apart from Miriam Courtney and Miss Simms, no one seemed to have left the room. When he looked up after half an hour, the place was empty apart from Mrs Freedman. 'Why Miss Simms and Mrs Bloxby?' he asked.

'I don't understand you,' said Mrs Freedman.

'No first names.'

'Oh, they're members of the Carsely Ladies' Society. It's an old-fashioned tradition. They don't use first names.'

Simon then focused on Tilly Glossop. She was reported to have been having an affair with Sunday. Had he been using that photograph of her with the mayor to get a bit of free sex for himself?

His stomach rumbled and he looked up at the clock in surprise. 'I'm just going out for lunch,' he said. 'Then tell them I've gone over to Odley Cruesis to have a look at the place. Can I get you anything?'

'No, I had a sandwich at my desk. Don't you think you should phone Mrs Raisin first and say you're going there?'

'I'll be on a motorbike with my helmet on. I just want to get a feel of the place.'

Simon went to the nearest Burger King and gulped down a hamburger and fries before getting on his bike and heading for Odley Cruesis. He drove carefully right through the village and parked up on a hill above it.

Visitors to the beauty spot that is the Cotswolds often pass by villages like Odley Cruesis, hidden down in a fold of the Cotswold hills. They go instead to the main tourist spots such as Chipping Campden or Bourton-on-the-Water or Stow-on-the-Wold.

The village was very quiet. A high wind soughed through the tops of the old elm trees surrounding the small triangle of village green. The little cottages that he could see were all very small and so covered in creeping plants of various varieties – wisteria, clematis and Virginia creeper – that the houses themselves seemed to have become part of the vegetation.

Simon approached the church and studied the notice-board. The notices announcing various events were mostly old and faded, but there was one new one, recently pinned up. It said, 'Room to let in period house of great charm. Contact Miss May Dinwoody.' Then followed the address and phone number.

He took out his mobile phone and called Agatha. When he had finished speaking, she squawked down the line, 'You want to live there? It could be dangerous. Not only have there been two murders but a friend of mine got struck on the head and ended up in hospital. And what on earth would be your excuse for living there?'

'My parents were both killed in a car crash – true. I want peace and quiet to recover from the trauma. I am interested in entering the Church.'

'Are you?'

'One visit to Mircester Library and I'll know an awful lot about it. I'm good at integrating myself.'

'All right. Give it a try and report to me every evening. We'll keep it secret. Don't come near the office. I'll tell everyone you've decided not to take the job. Have you enough money to put down a deposit?'

'Yes. I'm not going to rush into things so it could take some time. Can you remember exactly where she lives?'

'She lives in the old mill house. There's a track leads down the far side of the shop and you reach it that way.'

Simon glanced at the village shop as he passed. It looked a gloomy place with a tattered banner hanging over the door emblazoned with the legend: YOUR VILLAGE SHOP – USE IT OR LOSE IT. I'd better shop there, he thought. Probably think in this place that a visit to a supermarket amounts to treason. Funny. It doesn't feel calm and peaceful. I feel as if hundreds of eyes are watching me.

He made his way down a damp weedy track to where the old mill house brooded over a weedy pond. He pressed the bell to Flat 3 and a voice told him over the intercom to enter.

May Dinwoody's first words when she saw him sounded disappointed. 'I was hoping for someone older,' she said in her reedy voice. 'Maybe an elderly gentleman. There have been murders in this village and one feels so very frightened.'

Simon smiled. 'Maybe a young man would be better protection.'

'Oh, well, you'd best come in. Take a seat.'

Grey-haired May Dinwoody was wearing an odd assortment of clothes: a ratty brown cardigan over a red sequinned evening top, harem trousers and trainers.

'You had better give me references,' she said.

'I have with me,' said Simon, 'my school certificates and my driving licence. I do not have job references because I have never worked. My parents were killed in a car crash last year and it has taken me a long time to sort out their affairs with the lawyers. My home is 22, Blackberry Avenue, Mircester, but it is up for sale. I want to stay somewhere very quiet for a little while until I decide what I am going to do. I am seriously thinking of entering the Church.'

'I think you'll do very well,' said May. 'We'll have some coffee and go across to the vicarage so that you may meet the vicar. But first, I shall show you your room. It's a bit small. I'm afraid it doesn't overlook the pond. It really was the pond view that persuaded me to move here.'

How such a dank and murky pond could attract anyone was beyond Simon's imaginings, but he followed through to a room at the back. The room, although small, had a large window overlooking the village green. 'The previous tenant was an artist and he got that large window put in,' said May. 'Such desecration. He'd never have got planning permission these days.'

The room was simply furnished with a single bed, a wardrobe, a chest of drawers, a desk at the window and three hard chairs.

'Now, I'll show you the bathroom. I'm afraid I shall ask you to supply your own sheets and towels.'

'That's all right,' said Simon. 'Can manage that.'

'Now follow me. Off to the right of the living room is the kitchen. We'll need to share the fridge and shelves. I will keep my groceries on the bottom two shelves and you may have the top two shelves and one freezer drawer. The cupboard up here on the left is yours also.'

'Looks fine.'

'There is another room here but I use that as my workshop. I make toys.'

'How clever of you!'

May's voice began to tremble. 'There is now the question of the rent and the deposit.'

'How much?'

'Seventy-five pounds a week and three months in advance.'

'Okay. Cash or cheque?'

May blinked at him.

'If you said I was a nephew or something like that,' said Simon, 'I could pay you the cash and then you would not have to pay any taxes.'

'That would be criminal!'

Simon grinned. 'Yes, wouldn't it just!'

'Isn't it, well, a wee bit naughty?'

'Just a bit.'

'Oh, all right then,' said May. 'It's a good thing that John Sunday is dead. He'd soon have found something out.'

'I read about that. Perhaps before I meet the vicar I should go back to my place and collect my belongings and get you the money from the bank?'

'Yes, yes, of course,' twittered May.

'Am I supposed to be Scottish, like you?'

'I wouldn't bother. My poor sister, now dead, was married to an Englishman. They did not have any children, but nobody in the village knows that.'

Simon said goodbye and May sat down and stared out at the rippling waters of the millpond. She gained a little money from selling her toys at various fairs, but her pension did not stretch to much. Her last luxury was smoking and she thought day in and day out about giving it up. What if this odd-looking young man didn't come back?

But two hours later, Simon came back driving his father's old vintage Morris Minor. He felt it was more suitable than a motorbike to his image of a young man interested in the Church. He carried in a box of sheets and towels and pillowslips and then gave May an envelope full of money.

Simon went back to bring in a suitcase and while he was hanging his clothes away, he briefly regretted that he would not be seeing Toni for some time. Agatha Raisin appeared to be a rather formidable woman. Still, she was reported to have solved a lot of cases and it took an intelligent woman to do that.

Mircester market happened once a week in the little square in front of the abbey. Agatha loved poking around it, often buying tempting fresh fruit and vegetables which she never got around to eating and ended up giving away.

Then as she looked across the stalls, she saw Tom Courtney's sister, Amy Bairns. Her stomach gave a lurch. She was in no doubt as to what Amy was doing in the area. Hadn't escaped murderers, or in Amy's case, assistant murderers historically come back to wreak vengeance?

She edged her way round the stalls until she was behind the woman and grasped her firmly and began to scream, 'Police! Help!'

Two policemen on duty at the market rushed up. 'Leave me alone!' shouted Amy in an American accent. 'This woman's mad.'

'And this woman,' panted Agatha, 'is the sister of that murderer, Tom Courtney.'

The policemen took over. They handcuffed her and led her off with Agatha following.

Agatha was told to wait in the reception area of police headquarters. She felt elated with triumph.

After half an hour, a tall man strode up to the desk sergeant and demanded, 'What are you doing with my wife?'

'What is the name of your wife?'

'Maisie Berger. We're here on holiday and they tell me at the market that some woman started screaming at poor Maisie and Maisie was taken in here.'

The desk sergeant pressed the buzzer. 'If you will just come through, sir.'

A little lump of ice began to form in Agatha's stomach. She couldn't be wrong. Of course – they must have fake passports.

Another half hour dragged past. The plastic palm which decorated the waiting area was dusty. The cheerful noises from the market filtered in from the street. Several members of the press started to come in, demanding to know who had been arrested. They swung round and saw Agatha and were bearing down on her when Inspector Wilkes called, 'Mrs Raisin, if you will just come this way.'

Agatha was buzzed through and led into an interview room. As she sat down opposite Wilkes, she noticed first that he was alone, and second that the tape wasn't running.

'The woman you grabbed is exactly who she says she is,' said Wilkes. 'What on earth made you think she was Amy Bairns?'

'It was that Californian face-lift look, you know, they all look as if they came off the same alien planet.'

'We have given them full apologies and we are paying their hotel bill, plus a set of golf clubs for the husband and a week at a health spa for both of them so that they will not press charges. We will send you the bill for all this in return for us not arresting you for wasting police time. You will leave by the back door and you will not, repeat not, speak to the press. Get it?'

'Got it,' said Agatha miserably.

Wilkes' expression softened slightly. He had to admit that he too had received a shock when he had first seen Mrs Berger. She did look almost identical to the missing Amy Bairns.

'Go back to your usual run-of-the-mill detecting, Mrs Raisin. That will be all.'

He rang a bell and told the policewoman who answered the summons, 'Show Mrs Raisin out by the back way.'

When Agatha got back to the office, she said to Mrs Freedman, 'If there are any calls from the press, I'm not available.'

'There've been quite a few already,' said Mrs Freedman.

Patrick was helping himself to a cup of coffee. 'What's up?' he asked.

Agatha told him. She ending by exclaiming, 'How could I have been so stupid?'

Patrick looked at her for a long moment. Then he said, 'Did you ever see a photo of Dr Bairns?'

'No, why? Well, maybe I must have. I think there was a grainy photo in one of the newspapers I saw.'

'Let me check my computer,' said Patrick. 'I made contact with a chap in the Philadelphia police and he sent me some stuff over.'

'They must be who they say they are,' protested Agatha. 'They had passports and everything, I suppose.'

'Give me a few minutes. Have a cigarette and relax.'

Mrs Freedman gave a loud sigh as Agatha lit up a cigarette, and pointedly opened the window next to her desk as far as it would go.

'I'll lock the door,' said Agatha. 'I can hear the clump of press footsteps on the stairs.'

Patrick tapped away at the keys while Agatha ignored the ringing of the doorbell and the shouts through the letter box.

'Got it,' he said at last. 'Come and have a look.'

Agatha went over and studied the photograph on his computer. 'It's him!' she shouted. 'The man who said he was Berger. Which means he's Dr Bairns and she's Amy! Come on, Patrick. Print that off and we'll take it to Wilkes.'

* * *

141

'What is she up to now?' asked Wilkes when the desk sergeant phoned through to say Mrs Raisin and Patrick Mulligan were back with vital information and if he didn't see them quick, a murderer would get away. He had shut the press outside, but Mrs Raisin had promised them a statement after she saw Wilkes.

'I'll send someone to fetch her,' said Wilkes. 'But I think she's finally cracked.'

Detective Sergeant Collins appeared, her eyes gleaming with malice and her hair as usual pulled back so tightly into a bun that it made Agatha wonder why she didn't suffer from permanent headaches.

'You've done it this time, you silly old trout,' said Collins. 'The press will have a field day.'

'Oh, they will indeed,' said Agatha sweetly.

Wilkes met her in the corridor. 'Come in,' he snapped. 'What mad idea have you had now?'

Patrick and Agatha followed him into the interview room. 'Show him that photo, Patrick,' said Agatha.

Patrick put the printed-out photo on the desk in front of Wilkes. 'That,' said Agatha, 'is a photo of Dr Bairns, Amy Bairns's husband. Recognize the face?'

Wilkes shouted, 'Wait there!' and rushed from the room. They could hear him frantically shouting instructions. Agatha went to the window. Police were erupting out of the police station and heading off in the direction of the George Hotel. Other police cars were racing off. Patrick joined her.

'Just look at them,' he said. 'There's a funny quotation I heard once about a knight who jumped on his horse and rode off madly in all directions.'

'Why did Amy come here, of all places?' wondered Agatha.

'Probably thought it would be the last place anyone would expect to see her. Maybe she wanted revenge on you. She seems to be very close to her brother. Twins are usually close. They're probably long gone by now.'

'Did they never suspect the husband of having been in on it?'

'Not for a moment. Good Republican, contributes annually to the Philadelphian police fund. Model citizen.'

'I wonder why Tom Courtney wanted me to find out the murderer. Did he think I was such an amateur I'd never guess it was him?'

'Maybe he had such a high opinion of himself he thought you would fall for him.'

'Then he must be mad,' said Agatha, feeling a guilty flush rising to her cheeks.

'By God! Look! They've got them,' said Patrick. Amy and her husband were being marched across the square by a posse of police officers and detectives.

'It's time the agency got a bit of publicity.' Agatha grinned. 'Let's go out and meet the press.'

Patrick walked to the door and then turned round in surprise. 'It's locked!'

'They can't do this!' protested Agatha. 'They don't want me out there explaining what a fool the police made of themselves.'

She began to hammer on the door. It was finally unlocked and opened by Wilkes.

'I want you to leave again by the back door, Mrs Raisin,' he said. 'I will talk to the press.'

'If it hadn't been for me, you'd never have got them!' howled Agatha.

'Look, unless you leave quietly,' said Wilkes, 'I will make sure that you do not get any further help from us.'

'What! When have you ever helped me?'

'Do as you're told. Just go. Detective Sergeant Wong will escort you out.'

At the back exit, Agatha said furiously to Bill, 'I'm surprised at you, going along with this.'

'What do you expect me to do?' asked Bill. 'Disobey orders? Look, as soon as I can get away, I'll come to your home and tell you as much as I can.'

'I'm not going to creep away,' said Agatha when Bill had left. 'It's a free country. Let's go round the front and stand at the back of the crowd. I'd like to hear what Wilkes is going to say.'

The press were gathering outside. Wilkes was taking his time. More and more press began to arrive and a television van hurtled into the square and parked.

A crowd of onlookers crowded in along with the press. 'We'll just stand at the back,' said Agatha.

Agatha's feet were beginning to hurt as an hour passed and then another half hour before Wilkes appeared in front of police headquarters flanked by Chief Superintendent Jack Petrie on one side, and a beaming Detective Sergeant Collins on the other.

'This is only a brief statement,' said Wilkes. 'A man and woman have been arrested in connection with the murder of Miriam Courtney. There will be a further statement tomorrow. That is all. Thank you for waiting.'

'Just a minute!' cried a loud voice. Agatha stood on

tiptoe and recognized local reporter, Jimmy Torrance, pushing his way to the front. 'Detective Sergeant Collins told me earlier that private detective Agatha Raisin had made a right fool of herself by getting the wrong woman arrested. Was it the wrong woman or was she right all along?'

'I was right!' shouted Agatha.

The press turned round and began to surround her. Wilkes turned to Collins and said grimly, 'Follow me.'

Agatha, feeling that she had a legitimate reason to defend herself, gave the assembled press her version, carefully leaving out anything that might be regarded later as *sub judice*. She simply stated that she had recognized a woman whom she believed was a suspect in a murder case and had called on the police for help. She, Agatha, had subsequently been told she had made a terrible mistake but her detective, Patrick Mulligan, had found a photograph that proved she had been right all along. Agatha ended tactfully by saying they would need to contact the police for further details.

Chapter Eight

It was late that evening before Bill Wong arrived at Agatha's cottage. In her kitchen, he found waiting Toni, Patrick and Phil, all eager to hear his news.

'This is outside the call of duty,' said Bill wearily, 'but you have done me a great favour, Agatha. Collins has been suspended from duty. I hate that awful woman.'

'She'll get away with it,' said Agatha. 'She won't be the first detective to be caught off guard by a reporter.'

'Oh, it gets worse. Let me sit down, get me a coffee and I'll tell you what I can.'

Once he was settled at the kitchen table with a fresh cup of coffee, Bill began.

'Amy confessed to everything. She completely broke down. Her husband's alibi was false. Dressed as a man, she flew to the Cayman Islands as her brother while he, in the guise of a woman and under Mrs Temple's name, flew into London. He did the murder, flew back and then flew in again under his own name.'

'But why so elaborate a plot?' asked Agatha. 'I mean, they could have waited patiently until she visited the States and somehow made it look like a mugging.'

'Both brother and sister have records of mental breakdowns. Tom Courtney was believed to be a schizophrenic.'

'But if Tom Courtney's the murderer, why did he hire me?'

'He called at police headquarters and talked to Collins at one point. She did not report it. He told her he had received a phone call from his mother before her death, saying she had employed a private detective to look into Sunday's murder and who was this private detective? Collins had said that you were some sort of local menace who did more to impede the police in their inquiries than anything else. So he thought it would look good if he hired you as well, and yet not put himself at any risk.'

Agatha blushed. She had nearly gone to bed with a madman and murderer who thought she was a failure at her job.

'I know you're furious,' said Bill, taking her high colour for anger, 'but it was just another nail in Collins' coffin, I think. Still, it does seem certain that the Courtneys had nothing to do with the murder of Sunday, so we're back to square one on that case. Anyway, Amy considered the face change a good investment.'

'There are no plastic surgeons in prison,' said Toni. 'I wonder what she'll look like by the time the case gets to court. Oh, do you want me to start showing Simon the ropes? I haven't seen him today.'

'I've decided not to employ him,' lied Agatha, and then felt conscience-stricken as Toni gave a sad little 'Oh.'

'Why?' asked Phil. 'He seemed keen.'

'I don't feel like going into it at the moment,' said Agatha.

'Do you want me to start ferreting around Odley Cruesis?' asked Phil.

'*No!*' said Agatha, and, seeing the looks of surprise, said, 'Sorry I shouted at you but we've cases to clear up, and with this latest publicity we'll probably get a lot more. Has Tom Courtney been extradited yet?'

'Still waiting, but now we've got Amy, I suppose it won't be long.'

Bill's phone rang. He walked out of the room, shouting over his shoulder, 'Keep quiet, all of you. If Wilkes knew I was here, he would have a fit.'

He came back after only a few moments, saying, 'I've got to go. Full inquiry. They're dead.'

'Who?' asked a chorus of voices.

'Both of them, Amy and her husband. Took poison.'

'How did they get poison?' asked Agatha.

'They had cyanide in a button on each of their jackets. I'm off.'

'Snakes and bastards!' said Agatha. 'That wipes me out of the headlines.'

'Cheer up,' said Patrick. 'It's too late for the morning editions.'

'So it is! Champagne, anyone?'

On the following Sunday, Toni decided to go to church in Odley Cruesis. She could not understand why Agatha appeared to have lost interest in the case. She thought that a visit to the church when everyone thought things had all settled down might give her a feel of the place but remembering the attack on Roy Silver, she decided to go in disguise.

Agatha had a box of various disguises in the office. Toni let herself into the office with her key, found the box and selected a black wig and fitted it over her short blonde hair. The black wig transformed her appearance. She was wearing a conservative blue linen suit and flat heels. Toni surveyed herself in the mirror above the filing cabinets and thought she looked the very picture of a churchgoer.

It was a perfect day with the beauty of the rural Cotswolds stretched out under a large sky. Because of all the recent rain and the humid heat, the vegetation around was thicker than ever, turning the country lanes into green tunnels.

She was initially surprised to find the church was full but recognized what she considered to be a lot of visitors. No doubt the renewed publicity about Miriam's murder had bought out what Toni privately damned as 'the rubberneckers', people who always flocked to the scene of a murder or car crash out of ghoulish interest.

She sat in a pew at the very back of the church, and as the sermon went on, said a silent prayer for the soul of Sharon. Toni was not sure that she really believed in anything, but there was something tranquil about the old church, despite the influx of visitors, as if the very stones held memories of the peace they had brought to the worried and suffering over the centuries.

She stood up when the service ended and went out into the churchyard. Toni watched people leaving. She recognized Mrs Carrie Brother as she stopped to talk to the vicar. Then out came the two elderly couples, the Summers and the Beagles, followed after a short while by Tilly Glossop. Now hadn't Tilly been the one who had been photographed having sex with the mayor? She could do with some more investigating. And then came May Dinwoody, leaning on the arm of . . . Simon Black!

Then Penelope Timson appeared and spoke to Simon and May and led them off towards the vicarage. Simon said something and turned and ran back into the church. He came out a few moments later, passed close to Toni and dropped a piece of paper and then ran towards the vicarage.

Toni picked up the paper. 'Meet me on Dover's Hill at three this afternoon.'

Toni had visited Dover's Hill before to watch the annual Cotswold Olimpicks. The hill is a natural amphitheatre about one mile away from Chipping Campden. She remembered being particularly amused by the ancient sport of shin kicking, practised in Britain since the early seventeenth century. It was considered too painful a sport and was banished early in the twentieth century but brought back in 1951. Unlike the older games, where competitors used to harden their shins with hammers and wear iron-capped boots, the modern contestants wear long trousers with straw padding underneath. The trick is to wrestle your opponent to the ground while kicking him in the shins. Other sports included an obstacle race, falconry and morris dancing before the final torchlight procession to the square in Chipping Campden where everyone dances the night away.

That year's games had already been held in May. There were only a few tourists in the parking area at the top of Dover's Hill when Toni drove up – the world recession and a combination of the swine flu outbreak and the strong pound keeping most of them away.

She walked to the top of the amphitheatre and admired the view. Some people were having picnics on the grass. A very English smell of hot tea wafted up the hill.

She walked back to the car park and saw Simon driving up in an old Morris Minor. He signalled to her and she went to join him, climbing into the passenger seat.

'What are you doing in Odley?' asked Toni.

'I'm working undercover,' said Simon.

'With Agatha's permission?'

'Yes. She doesn't want anyone to know. I'm staying with May Dinwoody as a lodger. Don't tell Agatha you've seen me or I'll get my first black mark.'

'I won't, but what's your cover?'

'I'm taking time off after my parents' death and I am interested in early English church architecture. I told the vicar I couldn't stay for lunch as I had an urgent appointment and got out of there before he could ask what the appointment was.'

'How are you getting on?'

'Fine. Fortunately, Giles, the vicar, likes to hear the sound of his own voice. He preaches on and on, so all I have to do is listen. Then May Dinwoody makes toys to sell at the markets so I'm helping her. We'll be at Morton market on Tuesday.'

'Does anyone in the office know what you are doing?'

'No.'

'Then you'd better be careful. Sometimes, if it's quiet at the office, Phil Marshall goes shopping at the market. If I were you, I'd wear a hat and sunglasses, just in case. And talking of disguises, how on earth did you recognize me under this wig?'

Simon laughed. 'Once seen, never forgotten. Any hope of seeing you again?'

'I wouldn't like to at the moment. I just hope I haven't risked anything by meeting up with you.'

Simon glanced around. 'Nothing but tourists. Don't worry. I know – I might take next Sunday off, say I'm visiting relatives and meet you in Mircester.'

'I'll give you my phone number,' said Toni.

'I've already got it. I took it off the files in the office along with your mobile number.'

'So why didn't you just ring my mobile when you saw me in the graveyard?'

'Think about it, Toni. Everyone would have turned and had a look at you when your sacrilegious phone started ringing amongst the gravestones.'

'See you.' Toni got out of Simon's elderly car and got into her own. It was hot from the sun beating down on it. She opened the windows, took off the black wig and put it on the seat beside her. As she started up the engine and twisted her neck to reverse out, she had a funny feeling of being watched. She got out of the car again and looked around. Nothing but the usual tourists and a busload of pensioners on a day out from Wales. *Evans Luxury Tours, Cardiff* was emblazoned on the side of a bus that looked as decrepit as the passengers stiffly climbing back on board.

Toni was just about to drive off again when her mobile phone rang. It was Simon. 'In all the excitement of meeting you,' he said, 'I forgot to tell you about an awful article in the *Sunday Cable* about Agatha.'

Stopping at a newsagent's in Chipping Campden, Toni bought a copy of the *Sunday Cable*.

She skimmed through it until she came to a large head-and-shoulders photo of Agatha. The headline read: ENGLAND'S ANSWER TO INSPECTOR CLOUSEAU.

It was a cruelly funny article that started with Agatha's first attempt to marry James Lacey, which was aborted when her husband, whom she had presumed dead, turned up to stop the ceremony. Then followed details about how many times the police had had to rescue Agatha at great cost to the taxpayer. She was damned as an amateur who bumbled about from case to case, smoking, drinking and bullying until she frightened someone into attacking her. The author was a reporter called Dan Palmer.

Toni decided to go and see how Agatha was coping with this thunderbolt.

She met Charles on the doorstep. 'I am here to do a bit of hand-holding,' he said. 'Seen the article?'

Toni nodded. Charles rang the bell. There was no reply. Charles opened the letterbox and shouted through it, 'It's me, Charles, with Toni!'

They waited and then the door opened. 'Come in,'

said Agatha abruptly. 'I suppose you've both seen the *Cable*. Come through to the garden.'

Charles and Toni sat down in garden chairs. Agatha was wearing an old housedress and her face was not made up.

'Are you going to sue?' asked Charles.

'I can't. Every occasion when the police came to my rescue is correct, including that last one which involved Scotland Yard and the River Thames Police and the coastguard.'

'But the names he called you!' exclaimed Toni.

'You will note, he says "In my opinion . . ." Can't sue someone over an opinion.'

'What did you ever do to him?' asked Charles. 'No, don't turn your head away. Out with it!'

'Okay, it's like this. When I was doing PR for a swimwear company, I invited the press to the launch of the new line. For swimwear you get male reporters as well as female for obvious reasons. He was one of them. I caught him hiding behind a screen in the dressing rooms, holding a camera over the top and taking pictures of the models undressing. I knocked back the screen and got one of my own photographers to snap him. I sent the photo with a complaint to his editor. He was on the *Express* at the time and lost his job.'

'Was he supposed to take pictures like that?' asked Toni.

'No, it was for his own salacious amusement. He had a good photographer in the audience whose job was to get some pretty pictures for the paper's colour supplement. This could ruin me.'

'He seems like a perv,' said Toni. 'I know, let's get something on him.'

'How?'

'We're detectives, aren't we?' said Toni eagerly. 'Give me a few days in London, Agatha.'

'He'd recognize you,' said Agatha.

'I could go in disguise.'

'I'll go,' said Charles.

'But you're not a detective!' exclaimed Toni.

'I'm hurt. His photo's on the article. I'll recognize him. Anyway, I know more about the underside of London than can be dreamt of in your philosophy, Horatio.'

'Why are you calling her Horatio?' asked Agatha.

Charles went up to London on the following day, left his bag at his club and went to a less salubrious club in Beecham Place. The club for gentlemen was actually a cross between a hard-drinking club and a brothel.

He asked the barman if his friend, Tuppy, had been in. 'He usually calls in around now,' said the barman. Charles ordered a drink and waited. After ten minutes, Lord Patrick Dinovan, who was known to his friends as Tuppy, came in. He was a small grey man with a crumpled face. Charles always thought that Tuppy had the most forgettable appearance of anyone he knew.

He hailed Charles with delight. 'Take a pew, Tuppy,' said Charles. 'I want you to do something criminal for me.'

'Why not do it yourself?'

'I might be recognized.'

'What's in it for me?'

'Free shooting. The pheasant season will be here before you know it.'

Dan Palmer was drinking alone in the Horse Tavern, a riverside pub frequented by the staff of the *Cable*. He had a bad reputation for turning nasty after a few drinks and so his colleagues were giving him a wide berth. At last the fact that no one wanted to speak to him seeped into his drunken brain and with a snarl he tossed down his drink and walked outside. He had only lurched a few steps when he bumped into a small man.

'I say, I am sorry,' said the man. 'Let me make it up to you. Drink?'

'Not in there,' said Dan, jerking a thumb back at the pub.

'I've a room in a hotel near here and a good bottle of malt if you care to join me,' said Tuppy.

Dan's little eyes narrowed into slits. 'Not gay, are you?'

'Bite your tongue. Oh, forget it.'

But Dan thought of the free drink. He longed for more. 'Okay,' he said. 'What's your name?'

'John Danver.'

'Lead on.'

The hotel was small but expensive looking. Dan sank down in an armchair in Tuppy's suite and gratefully accepted a large glass of malt.

'You're that famous reporter, Dan Palmer, aren't you?' asked Tuppy.

'That's me.'

'Tell me some of your best stories. I'm fascinated.'

Dan almost forgot to drink in his eagerness to brag. When he had finished, Tuppy said, 'Is that detective female, Raisin, really that stupid?'

Dan made to tap the side of his nose but drunkenly stuck his finger in his eye by mistake. 'Ouch!' he yelped. 'Oh, her, Aggie Raisin. No, that one's as cunning as a fox.'

'So why wreck her reputation?'

'I had an old score to pay back. Did that hatchet job pretty nicely, hey? There's nothing in there she can sue me about.'

'So she really is good?'

'Sure she is. That's what makes it funnier.'

'I don't understand . . . Your glass is empty, let me top it up. Do you mean if one of you reporters on the *Cable* wants revenge, they can write a piece to get it?'

'Only if they're as clever as me.'

'So your editor never guessed you were paying off an old score?'

'Him? He wouldn't know his arse from a hole in the ground.'

'He must be pretty good at his job to become editor, don't you think?'

'Hopeless. I could do the job better with both hands tied behind my back. He married the proprietor's niece. Shee! Thash how he got the post. You have to be as shmart as me to keep on top. Ish a jungle out there. Jungle!'

Dan rambled on and then suddenly fell asleep.

Tuppy removed the whisky glass from his hand. He switched off the powerful little tape recorder he had hidden behind a bowl of flowers on the table between them.

He made his way downstairs, pulling a baseball cap with a long peak out of his pocket and jamming it down on his head so that the peak shielded his face. He had sent a messenger to book the room under the name of Dan Palmer and pay cash in advance, plus a deposit. The foyer was still busy with a party of guests who had just entered. When he had arrived with Dan, the desk clerk had been on the phone and had not taken any particular notice of either Tuppy or Dan, and Tuppy had taken the precaution of keeping his room key with him.

Dan awoke at six in the morning with a blinding hangover. He struggled to his feet and made his way downstairs and out onto the street and hailed a taxi to take him to his digs, thanking his stars it was his day off.

He set out for the office on the following day, stopping at the local newsagent's to buy a copy of the *Cable*. A square box, outlined in black and with the headline APOLOGY, caught his eye.

He read, 'The *Cable* offers a full and complete apology to private detective Miss Agatha Raisin of the Raisin Detective Agency in Mircester over a recently published and misleading article, and wishes to assure readers that Miss Raisin is one of the country's foremost private detectives.'

What on earth ... ? He hailed a cab, got to the office and rushed up to the editorial floor, to be met by the editor's secretary. 'Mr Dixon would like a word with you.'

He trailed after her to the editor's office. Dixon was a thickset man with thinning hair and a pugnacious face. His office was flooded with the sunlight that was sparkling on the waters of the Thames outside the window.

'Listen to this,' said Dixon and switched on a tape recorder on his desk.

Dan listened in horror to that conversation he had had with that man who had called himself John Danver.

'I was set up,' he gasped.

'We were lucky to get away with only an apology. That Raisin woman could have sued our socks off. Now, in the past we've allowed you to write the occasional feature, but I've checked back on your work. Your few features always seem to skim this side of libellous. You can go and clear your desk. You're finished.'

'But . . .'

'Do you want me to call security?'

Dan went back to the hotel, only to be told that he had booked the room himself. He had stopped off on the way to have several drinks. He was told firmly that the room had been booked under his name and they could not tell him anything further. They would pay his deposit back.

Dan hated Agatha Raisin as he had never hated anyone before.

Charles regretted having offered Tuppy free shooting. After all, he depended on the pheasant season to raise money for his estate. Also, he had paid Tuppy for the hotel room and the malt whisky.

He interrupted Agatha's thanks by saying, 'I'm afraid it cost a lot of money – bribes and things.'

'How much?'

'Five thousand pounds.'

'Good heavens! Oh, well . . .' Agatha fished out her cheque book, wrote him out a cheque for the amount and handed it over. 'Are you staying at my place?'

'No, got things to do, people to see.' Charles felt a bit grubby, but money was money and estates like his just seemed to drink it up. 'Tell you what, I'll take you to lunch to celebrate.'

'Can't,' said Agatha. 'Got an important date.'

'You look shifty. Who with?'

'Mind your own business.'

Agatha's lunch date was in Evesham with Simon Black. Because of the recession, Evesham looked more depressed than ever. They met in a Thai restaurant in the High Street.

When they had ordered, Agatha asked, 'How are you getting on?'

'Slowly. You see,' said Simon, 'in a village like Odley Cruesis, unless you were born there, you'll always be an outsider. They're a secretive lot. The vicar loves his church more than God or his wife. I've admired the perpendicular north doorway for the umpteenth time, not to mention the Norman pulpit.'

'How are you getting on with May Dinwoody?'

'Pretty well. But she won't talk about John Sunday and neither will any of the other villagers. They're nice to me because I'm the vicar's pet. They talk about the weather and the crops mostly. I was in the store and I raised the subject of Sunday's murder. There was a little silence and then they began to talk about something else. Sometimes I think they could all have been in on it.

'I've been encouraging May to have some wine with her supper to see if that loosens her tongue.'

'What about Penelope Timson?' asked Agatha. 'Anything there?'

'She is one nervous and flustered lady. She keeps hugging me, although it feels like groping, and says I am the sort of son she would like to have.'

'Be careful,' warned Agatha. 'Give it another week and then clear out.'

That evening, Simon urged May to take a third glass of wine but she shook her head. 'I've had enough. I don't want to turn into a drunk. Oh, I quite forgot. The vicar wants you to report to the vicarage at nine in the morning. He thinks it's time you started helping with the parish duties.'

'But it's not as if I'm employed by the parish,' protested Simon.

'Oh, but it's not healthy for a young man of your age to do nothing. And you have shown such an interest in the Church – so rare these days. You will notice that we do not have many young people in the village. We have children but not teenagers.'

Probably got out of the damn place as soon as they could, thought Simon. Aloud, he asked, 'What am I supposed to be doing?'

'I think driving someone somewhere.'

When Simon rang the bell at the vicarage next morning, the vicar hailed him cheerily. 'Just the fellow! Mr and Mrs Summers and Mr and Mrs Beagle will be here shortly. They want to take a shopping trip to Cheltenham.'

'I don't think for a minute they'll all fit into my car,' said Simon.

'You can drive my people carrier. It's big enough for all of you. Ah, here they come. You might like to take them for a modest meal and I will refund you.'

The vicar tenderly helped the couples into the vehicle. The day was sunny and warm but they all seemed to be well wrapped up.

'Lovely day,' said Simon.

Silence.

'Why don't we all sing?' suggested Simon, unnerved by the brooding atmosphere.

'Shut up and drive,' growled Fred Summer, 'and keep your eyes on the road.'

It seemed to take ages to reach Cheltenham. Elderly bladders meant frequent stops.

Cheltenham was the site of a monastery as early as 803. Alfred the Great admired the peace of the place, but the town's sudden rise began in the eighteenth century with the discovery of the famous spa waters. People like

Handel and Samuel Johnson flocked to the town to take the restorative cure.

Simon drove into the Evesham Road car park. He had to let his elderly cargo out before he parked because the parking places there were so small that every vehicle seemed to have just squeezed its way in.

He caught up with the two couples as they shuffled their way out of the car park. 'Here, you,' said Fred. 'You ain't coming with us. Meet us back here at five o'clock.'

'But I'm supposed to take you to lunch,' said Simon.

'Us'll get our own lunch and charge the vicar. Shove off.'

Simon glanced at his watch. It was only half past ten in the morning. Perhaps Toni could join him. He phoned her mobile.

'Toni,' he began eagerly. 'Simon here.'

'Oh, hello, Lucy,' said Toni brightly. 'I'm in the office.'

'I'm stuck in Cheltenham. If you can get away for lunch, I'll meet you at that pasta place on the Parade at one.'

'I'll try. Got to go.'

After he had rung off, Simon realized he wasn't much of a detective. Anyone from the village was surely a suspect. He should have followed his passengers and seen what they were up to. They walked so slowly, they couldn't possibly have got far. But as he raced down the slope into the centre of the town, he could not see them.

He stopped his search when he realized how idiotic he was being. His four passengers had been inside the vicarage drawing room when the murder had been committed.

He passed a pleasant time looking around the shops and then made his way to the restaurant on the Parade, where he hoped to meet Toni. He managed to secure a table outside, ordered a glass of lager and said he would order the meal when his friend arrived.

Fifteen minutes later, he had just decided she would not be able to come when he saw her bright golden hair and slim figure heading towards him through the crowd.

'Hi!' said Toni. 'What are you doing in Cheltenham? I thought you were stuck in that village looking for suspects.'

'I got stuck with running four of the crinklies here for the day.'

'Which four?'

'The Summers and the Beagles.'

Toni leapt to her feet, nearly colliding with the hovering waiter. 'You idiot!' she said. 'They know what I look like. Your cover'll be blown if they see you here with me.' And she was off and running.

Simon watched miserably as her fair head bobbed up and down as she ran through the crowd and then disappeared from view. Simon gloomily ordered a toasted cheese baguette. He felt every bit the idiot Toni had called him. He found her very attractive, but if he was going to make any success of this job, he'd better keep his mind strictly on it until he found out something useful. The only person in the village who seemed prepared to gossip to him was May Dinwoody. The likeliest subject was Tilly Glossop. She had had an affair, as far as anyone knew, with Sunday. He had a photograph of her in a compromising position with the mayor. Nothing of her affair with the mayor had leaked into the press.

He could only assume that the whole business had been hushed up. In the report which Simon had accessed, Patrick had said that Tilly had claimed it was a brief fling and there was nothing in the mayor's bank statements that revealed he was being blackmailed. How had Sunday got hold of the photo? Tilly swore she did not know.

I must manage to get friendly with Tilly, thought Simon, as he passed a slow afternoon and eventually made his way back to the car park in time to pick up his passengers.

His charges arrived promptly at five o'clock, carrying various plastic shopping bags. He gathered from their conversation – for not one of them addressed him directly – that apart from shopping they had been 'taking the waters'.

On the road back to the village there had to be even more 'comfort stops' than there had been on the road in, so it was dark by the time he thankfully reached the village and helped them out of the people carrier, before taking it back to the vicarage and leaving it outside.

Either his imagination was working overtime or Odley Cruesis was an eerie place. As he made his way across the village green and along the lane to the old mill house, it was completely silent. No dog barked, no voices sounded in the still summer air, not even the blare of a television set.

He sighed. Another evening of polite conversation with May. If only he could find out something, anything, to enable him to get out of this place. There was a large yellow moon in the sky, turning the waters of the old millpond to gold.

He stood at the edge of the pond, looking at the water. A vicious shove right between the shoulder blades sent him hurtling down into the pool.

Something prompted him to stay down as long as possible. His terrified mind conjured up visions of medieval-type villagers with pickaxes and billhooks waiting for him to surface. At last, he thrust himself upwards, shaking the water from his eyes and casting terrified looks around but there was no one there. He hauled himself up the steep bank and lay panting on the grass.

Instead of going to the mill house, he ran to his car and drove as fast as he could to Agatha's cottage in Carsely.

Agatha answered the door and stared in amazement at the soaking figure of Simon. 'Come in,' she said. 'What on earth happened?'

Simon told her about the attack on him. 'I'm a good swimmer,' he said, 'otherwise I would have drowned.'

'I'll run you a hot bath,' said Agatha. 'My friend, Charles, has left a dressing gown and some clothes in the spare room. Brandy? Maybe not. Hot sweet tea is the answer.'

'I know,' said Simon, 'but I'd rather have the brandy.'

'Leave your clothes outside the bathroom and I'll put

them in the tumble dryer. Good thing you were only wearing a shirt and trousers and not your best suit.'

After Simon had bathed and was dressed in Charles' dressing gown and was waiting for his clothes to dry, Agatha said, 'Well, that's you finished with that village. What did you do today?'

So Simon told her but could not admit he had seen Toni. Yet someone must have seen him. Perhaps the old people. Even so, surely they hadn't had any time to gossip to anyone in the village. Of course they could always have phoned someone. But he said none of this aloud.

'I want you to type out every little thing you can think of,' said Agatha. 'Describe your stay at the village from beginning to end, what people said, what impression you had of them. I suppose they all hope that Tom Courtney for some odd reason killed Sunday himself. You may know more than you think you know. Take the whole day tomorrow to do it. I'll break it to the others that you were employed by me after all. Now, do we report this to the police? No, they'll start raging about us interfering. You'd better phone May Dinwoody and tell her that you're visiting a friend and then you're moving out. I know, I'll phone her and say I am your aunt. I'm very good at accents.'

Agatha phoned May and adopted what she cheerfully thought was a Gloucestershire accent. After she had finished calling, she told Simon cheerfully, 'She's a bit upset about losing you. Do you want me to get Patrick or Phil to go and collect your stuff? It does seem as if someone in that cursed village guessed you were work-ing for me.'

'No, I'll go myself,' said Simon. 'May and I got very friendly. I don't want her to know.'

'If you like. But I would go as soon as your clothes are dry, because I bet the gossip will be all round the village by the morning.'

On his return to the mill house, Simon discovered that Agatha's fond interpretation of a Gloucestershire accent had not fooled May one bit. 'It was that Raisin female,' she said. 'I recognized that bullying voice of hers the minute she spoke.'

Chapter Nine

May listened while Simon told her how someone had pushed him into the millpond.

'You've only yourself to blame,' said May. 'This is a nice village. You'll find the murderer was that Tom Courtney. One of the village boys must just have been playing a wee joke on you.'

'I haven't seen any boys around,' protested Simon. 'Everyone seems pretty old to me.'

May bristled with outrage. 'You're not much of a detective, are you? We have a few boys and girls who are bussed over to the school at Chipping Campden.'

Simon suddenly remembered the vicar asking him if he could swim. Not wanting to be drawn into any village activities, he had said he could not. Penelope had been there.

'Anyway, just you pack your things up, laddie, and leave now. I don't like cheats.'

Simon mumbled an apology and went off to pack.

The next day found Agatha Raisin in a militant mood. Firstly, she was annoyed that her famous accent hadn't worked, and secondly, she decided it was time she went back to that village with Toni and Patrick to start the questioning all over again.

Patrick had told her through his police contacts that the office end of John Sunday's life had been thoroughly investigated and nothing sinister had been found. Tilly Glossop had been questioned over and over again but they could get nothing further out of her. Sunday, apart from the photograph of the mayor, had several e-mails from staff members he had printed off. Each contained something they would not like the boss or the wife or husband to know but they all had cast-iron alibis for the time of Sunday's death. Sunday, it appeared, had not been a blackmailer, merely using his knowledge as power to do what he liked in his job.

Agatha thought guiltily of that compromising photo of Penelope Timson. She should never have suppressed it.

When they arrived in the village, she decided to visit Penelope herself. Patrick was sent to see if he could get anything at all out of Tilly Glossop and Toni was dispatched to Carrie Brother.

Toni had been glad to see Simon back in the office. Agatha had briefly outlined his adventures. She wondered what her old school friends would make of Simon. With his beaky nose and long mouth, he looked a bit like a Bavarian puppet. But it was his warm smile and the way his dark eyes sparkled under his thick thatch of curly black hair that made her find him endearing. And he had been kind to her.

Toni rang the bell of Carrie's cottage and listened to

the cacophony of barking from Carrie's tape recorder before the lady herself opened the door. Her large face was blotched with tears.

'What's the matter?' exclaimed Toni. 'Is there anything I can do to help?'

'Yes, there is. Come in.'

Toni followed her into her cluttered parlour which still smelled of dog. Carrie rounded on her. 'You're a detective. I want you to solve a murder.'

'But that's why we're here.'

'I'm not talking about that snoop, Sunday, who deserved to die. I'm talking about my Pooky.'

'Pooky?'

'My little dog, my precious boy.'

'What happened?'

'It was yesterday. I was out on the village green and put Pooky down so that he could have a little run around. I saw him get hold of something and start eating it. By the time I got to him, he had finished it, whatever it was. I said, "Pooky, bad boy. You're not supposed to eat anything that Mummy doesn't give you."' Her eyes filled with tears. 'And Pooky just licked my nose and looked up at me with his little eyes. I took him home and put him in his basket. I went for an afternoon nap myself and when I woke up, he was dead! I took the body to the vet and demanded an autopsy.'

'Have you had the result?'

'Not yet. The stupid vet tried to tell me it was probably the result of overeating and not enough exercise.'

'How old was Pooky?'

'Nearly twelve years.'

'It's a good age for a dog.'

'Nonsense. He had years left in him.'

'Please sit down and let me make you a cup of tea,' urged Toni. 'You've had a bad shock.'

Without waiting for an answer, Toni found the kitchen and made a cup of strong sweet tea and took it back to Carrie. Carrie swallowed a gulp of tea and then said gruffly, 'You're a kind girl. No one else seems to care. They said that my Pooky fouled the village green.'

'If your dog was poisoned, who could have done it?'

'Any one of them could have done it. This was a nice village. Oh, we were all fed up with Sunday snooping around but it drew us closer together. While we had our little rows now and then, we were a close-knit community. Even Miriam fitted in. We let her play lady of the manor because she did a lot for the village. For a while, everything was back to normal because people were sure Tom Courtney had done it, but now it seems as if he couldn't and we have a murderer amongst us.'

'Who do you think could have killed Sunday? I mean, perhaps it might turn out to be the same person who killed your dog.'

Carrie looked steadily at Toni for a long moment, her eyes red-rimmed with weeping. 'I'll tell you,' she said at last. 'It was the vicar, Giles Timson.'

'But why?'

'He wouldn't let me bring Pooky to church. "What about all things bright and beautiful, all creatures great and small?" I asked him. And he sneered at me and said God created things like pythons and cockroaches. Now, would I want any of those in the church? And Pooky bit

172

his hand. And you should have seen the evil look he gave me. Besides,' – she lowered her voice – 'I saw his wife in a coffee shop in Mircester with John Sunday, and she was crying as if he were breaking up with her.'

Probably the photograph, thought Toni. 'Here is my card,' said Toni. 'Phone me the minute you get the result of the autopsy.'

Agatha found Penelope in the churchyard, clearing grass and long weeds away from the base of some of the old tombstones. She was wearing a pink straw hat with a wide brim and with pink and white dotted net wrapped around the crown.

'Splendid hat,' commented Agatha.

'Oh, this.' Penelope straightened up and pushed it to the back of her head. 'I only use it for gardening. I hate it. I bought it to wear at someone's wedding, some-one I really didn't like, so I never felt again like wearing this hat for dressing up. Silly, I know. Did you want something?'

Toni had phoned Agatha while Agatha had been searching around the vicarage for Penelope.

'I heard there was a young man staying here with May Dinwoody. Someone pushed him into the pond last night.'

'Simon? Such a nice young man. Why would anyone do that? Probably just a joke.' She lowered her voice. 'There are people in this village *who drink too much.*'

'Or someone who thought he could not swim,' said Agatha. 'What I really wanted to ask you was this. Look, it seems you were once seen in a café in Mircester with Sunday. Was it about that photo? What did he really want? Money? Tell the truth this time. He had that photo, didn't he?'

'Yes, but he didn't want money. Giles had bought a plot of land outside the village some time ago. He said when he retired, we could build a house there. I didn't want to go on living in the village. I'm a town person myself.'

'Which town?'

'I'm from Moreton-in-Marsh originally.' Hardly a buzzing metropolis, thought Agatha.

'So what did Sunday want? The building plot?'

'Yes, he wanted me to persuade Giles to sell it to him or he would send that photo to Giles.'

'When was this?'

'A week before the murder.'

'Why on earth would he want to live in Odley Cruesis?' asked Agatha.

'I think,' said Penelope, passing an earthy hand over her face and leaving streaks, 'that he wanted to build up a little microcosm of power. He liked bullying people.'

'So what did you do?'

'I invited him to tea and let him ask Giles if he could buy the plot. Giles refused point-blank. He asked Giles if he had a happy marriage. Giles gave him a curt yes, and John laughed and said, "Enjoy it while it lasts."

'I actually fantasized about killing him. That was when I told Giles about the photo. Do you really need to find out who did this murder? Are you sure it wasn't Tom Courtney?'

'Absolutely sure. And look at it this way. If the murderer is never found, you'll all go on suspecting each other and this village will never be the same again. If it ever was much to write home about in the first place.'

'Oh, it was lovely and peaceful and we all got along. Boring at times, of course.' Penelope took off the offending hat and put it on the head of a stone angel. 'And one could always go into Mircester for some culture. Did you see the local company's production of *The Marriage of Figaro* last year?'

Agatha had seen it in an attempt to widen her horizons but had disliked it so much that she put it down to her tin ear. She didn't know it had truly been dreadful, mainly because the role of Cherubino had been taken by the local newspaper editor's wife, which had ensured that the production received a glowing review despite the fact that Cherubino had a voice that could strip lead off a church roof.

'Yes,' said Agatha.

'So uplifting.'

'Just so. But we are getting away from the main subject. Think back to the evening Sunday was murdered. Are you absolutely sure no one left the room apart from Miriam and Miss Simms?'

'No one I can remember. But there was such a lot of smoke from the fire and I had to go out at one point to get the brandy.'

'Neither Tilly Glossop nor Carrie Brother attended.'

'Penelope!' shouted a voice from the vicarage.

175

'My husband. I must go.' Penelope fled, leaving her hat on top of the angel.

To his surprise, Patrick found that Tilly Glossop was actually flirting with him. When she served him a mug of coffee, she stretched round him, leaning her heavy breast against his shoulder. He could not quite remember any female flirting with him during his last twenty years, when his face had settled into its present lugubrious lines, but he smiled and tried to look flattered.

'So nice to have a man in the house,' said Tilly as she jangled over the coffee table. She had multiple bracelets on her thick wrists and chains with dangling bobbly objects around her neck. She was wearing a long, floating gown of some sort of chiffon material, semi-transparent, but enough to show she was wearing a formidable brassiere underneath and a pair of purple French knickers. 'Do try one of my cakes.'

'We're still interested in the Sunday murder,' said Patrick. 'You, having been closest to him, might have heard that someone was threatening him.'

Patrick had seen a woman's lips pout before, but Tilly's whole face seemed to pout, fat and wrinkles all creased forward.

'Nobody liked him much,' she said, plumping herself down on the sofa next to Patrick and releasing a cloud of scent.

'But you were heard to quarrel.'

'Oh, that was because I told him I had finished with

him,' said Tilly. 'He was amusing for a time, but that's me – easy come, easy go.'

How did she do it? wondered Patrick. She'd need to be the last woman on earth for me to ever dream of fancying her. 'I thought it was the other way round,' he ventured.

'Then you were wrong. Most people in the village had it in for him. But the atmosphere of the village had changed before he came.'

'How? Why?'

'This isn't an Agatha Christie-type village with some lord or some retired colonel at the head of the hierarchy, with the rest of us peasants waiting for an invitation to some fête in the manor grounds. We're all pretty equal. Old George Briggs used to own the manor, but he kept himself to himself. Then Miriam came and wanted to play lady of the village. It upset the balance, see? So folk were already edgy when Sunday came on the scene. Although there was all that fuss about the special ramp for the disabled at the manor and that turned her against him, I think she encouraged his petty little vendettas. She clashed with Giles, the vicar, a lot. She said the church was too *high*, all bells and smells, and the only reason for it was because he liked dressing up in all those fancy robes. But she did contribute to the church, although I'd swear that man hated her. Hell of a temper.'

Patrick wondered if all this was one hell of a red herring. 'What about that photograph of you and the mayor? You must know who took it.'

'It was Sunday. Too many complaints were coming in against him and the mayor had been swearing to do something about it.'

'So you set him up!'

'Not me. I told Sunday I was going to have a little fling with him when the mayor's missus was away, that was all. You can't blame me.'

Her cloying scent and proximity were beginning to make him feel queasy. 'Someone must be living in this village who is a murderer,' he persevered. 'There was that attack on Mrs Raisin's friend, Roy Silver. It could have killed him if it hadn't turned out he had a hard head.'

'I don't think that was attempted murder,' said Tilly. 'Probably someone just got fed up with that outside nosey parker. Can't we talk about something else?' She leaned against him.

Patrick got abruptly to his feet. 'Thank you for your time. I must be on my way.'

He moved rapidly for such a big man and before plump Tilly could struggle out of the depths of the sofa, she heard the front door slam behind him.

Patrick, Toni and Agatha met up on the village green. Only one of them had found out anything and that was that Tilly had told Sunday about her proposed fling with the mayor. Suddenly a clod of earth struck Agatha on the cheek. She swung round in a rage. She had not noticed any teenagers in the village before, but now there was a group of them, seizing stones and tussocks of earth and throwing them viciously, screaming, 'Get out! You ain't wanted here!'

They ran to their cars and met up again at the office. 'Do we report them to the police?' asked Toni.

'I don't think we should,' said Agatha. 'But as I ran to the car, I saw Giles, the vicar, looking out of the vicarage window. He made no move to run out and stop those boys. Well, let's get on with our other cases and forget Sunday for a bit. How are you getting on, Simon?'

Simon swung round in his chair. 'I've printed out all my notes. You told me to put in everything, no matter how small.'

'Great. I'll go over them later. No one is now paying us to find out who murdered Sunday, so we all need to begin to concentrate on our paying clients.'

When Agatha returned to her cottage that evening, she found Charles waiting for her. 'I've got something to report,' he said.

'About Sunday?'

'Forget Sunday. I was driving through Moreton-in-Marsh and who should I see walking boldly along the street but Dan Palmer?'

'I wonder what he's doing here?'

'Let's just hope he isn't looking for revenge. I heard through my contacts that he'd lost his job. I thought I'd keep you company just to be sure. How's the Sunday business going anyway?'

Agatha gave him the latest news. She ended with, 'I think this is one case that's never going to be solved.'

Dan Palmer craved a drink but he promised himself one later in the day, just one. He had taken notes of Agatha's cases with him before he had left the newspaper office and found the unsolved case of John Sunday. It was then he had a great idea. If he could solve the case, then he would set himself up as a private detective in competition with Agatha Raisin. He knew if he stayed sober, he could beat her hands down because he was prepared to use some dirty tricks that she probably wouldn't even contemplate.

He decided the best time would be around ten o'clock in the evening. He had a high-powered listening device. All he had to do was wait until everything was quiet and listen in to various conversations in the cottages. An old police contact had told him that the police were sure the murderer was one of the villagers.

He checked into a motel on the outskirts of Mircester on the ring road. There was no minibar in the room. He drove to a roadside restaurant and ate an all-day breakfast and felt better, although there was still a great hole inside him needing to be filled with alcohol. Just one drink wouldn't hurt.

At a pub in Mircester, he confined himself to two large vodkas. With a great effort, he got off the bar stool and back to his car, where he switched on the overhead light and studied an ordnance survey map until he located the road to Odley Cruesis.

The village was dark and silent. The little cottages around the green seemed to be crouching there. He drove out of the village and parked his car under a large horse chestnut tree on the crest of a hill. The sky was overcast. Clutching his listening device, which had cost him a fortune but had been the source of many scoops, he cautiously made his way back to the churchyard on foot, crouched behind a large tombstone, switched on the device and pointed it at the vicarage.

A man's voice came over, loud and clear. He cursed and turned down the sound so that only he could hear it. Must be the vicar. 'I'm off to bed,' he said. 'Coming?'

'In a minute, dear,' came a woman's voice. 'Just finishing the dishes.'

And that was that.

Great, just great, he thought. Let's try somewhere else. He was wearing dark clothes with a dark wool hat pulled down over his eyes. The evening was warm and humid and he was beginning to sweat. He emerged cautiously from behind his tombstone and then let out a scream. A tall hatted figure was staring down at him.

By the time he had recovered enough to see it was a stone angel with a hat on top, the vicarage door had opened and a tremulous woman's voice demanded, 'Anyone there?'

He crouched down again, his heart thudding, until she closed the door. He crept off. Down in the village, lights were shining from a tall building. He made his way there. A little road leading to the building had a sign saying Mill House Lane.

Crouching in bushes by the side of the pond, he

switched on the powerful listening device. 'I wish that young man hadn't left,' said a woman's voice. 'He was so nice. I'm sorry he turned out to be a snoop. The rent made such a difference. It's a bit hard to make ends meet these days and—'

A savage blow struck Dan on the back of the neck. He fell forwards. The listening device was picked up and thrown into the golden ripples of the moonlit pond.

Two days later, when Agatha was about to shut up the office for the evening, she received a visit from a Mrs Ruby Palmer.

She was a small, crushed-looking woman with mousy brown hair in tight permed curls. Her weak eyes blinked rapidly. She was wearing a droopy green cardigan over a cotton blouse of violent-coloured zigzags and a long white cotton skirt.

'I'm Dan's wife,' she said.

'You mean Dan Palmer? I'm sorry, Mrs Palmer, but if you've come to give me a row about your husband losing his job, forget it.'

'No, it's not that. You *are* a detective?'

'That's what it says on the door.'

'I need your help. Dan's gone missing.'

'He did drink a lot, Mrs Palmer. Maybe he's sleeping it off somewhere.'

'It's not that. He had this idea of outdoing you as a detective. He said he was going to go to that village and find that murderer. You see, he had this illegal listening device. The newspaper didn't know about it. You can stand outside people's houses and hear what they are saying. I would like to employ you to find him. Not that I miss him, mind you, because he was really nasty when he had taken drink. But he recently inherited a good bit of money from an uncle. He paid me only a little house-keeping money. If anything's happened to him, I won't get the money until they find his body. I filed a missing person's report with the police in Hackney but they weren't much interested.'

'All right,' said Agatha. 'I won't charge you unless I find him. Have you a card?'

Ruby produced a card from her shabby handbag.

'Are you staying in Mircester?'

'No, I'm driving back to Hackney.'

'That's quite a drive.'

'I'm used to it. Dan was usually too drunk to drive.'

'What kind of car does he drive?'

'An old Volvo.'

'Here's a piece of paper. Write down the registration number. Good. I'll be in touch as soon as I find out anything.'

When she had gone, Agatha began to phone round to all the hotels in the neighbourhood, at last hitting on the motel where Dan Palmer had last stayed. The desk clerk said he had not returned and if he was not back by the following day, they were going to pack up his things and leave them in the hotel storage room.

Agatha introduced herself and told them to leave the room as it could be a police matter.

She then phoned Simon and asked him if he would like to work late. 'I don't want to call the police in at this juncture because Palmer is such a drunk, he may have forgotten which hotel he was staying at. I want you to go and park outside and wait and see if he returns. Give it until about midnight.

'I'll stay here and start to phone round the pubs. Find out if he had a minibar in his room and then phone me back. If he didn't, I'm sure he would be feeling thirsty.'

After half an hour, Simon phoned back to say there was no minibar.

Agatha diligently began to phone round all the pubs in and around Mircester, but Dan Palmer could have passed in any crowd unnoticed. She bit her thumb in vexation. If he did not show up that evening, then she really would have to tell the police what he had been up to.

By midnight, Simon called to say there was no sign of the missing reporter.

Reluctantly, Agatha phoned Bill Wong at his home, to be told by his mother that Bill was working nights.

She locked up the office and made her way to police headquarters and asked for Bill, saying she had vital information in a murder case.

Bill came out and led her through into an interview room. It was more like a hotel lounge with comfortable chairs and magazines.

'Have you gone people friendly?' asked Agatha, looking around.

'We needed somewhere comfortable for the rape victims, abused children, cases like that. So, out with it. What's going on?'

184

Agatha described everything Ruby had told her. Bill took rapid notes. Then he said, 'You look worn out. Leave this to us.'

'But keep in touch with me,' said Agatha. 'After all, you'd never have known if I hadn't told you.'

'I promise.'

Chapter Ten

The next morning, Agatha said to Simon and Toni, 'You've heard all about how Dan Palmer is missing. I want you both to go to that wretched village and start to search. You won't be in any danger because the place will be crawling with police.'

Agatha did not know that Wilkes had turned down flat any idea of a search. 'He's a reporter and a drunk and a grown man,' Wilkes had said. 'I'm not wasting the manpower.'

So when Toni and Simon arrived, it was to find that there was not one policeman in sight. 'Well, it's a bright sunny day,' said Simon. 'They'll hardly attack us during daylight. Let's start looking. We need to find the car first.'

But there was no sign of Palmer's Volvo either in or around the village.

'Let's go and speak to May Dinwoody,' suggested Simon. 'I know she was angry with me, but I think she'll still have a soft spot for me and might have seen something.'

The lane to the mill house was still damp as it was overshadowed by trees and had not dried up after the recent rain. 'Look,' said Toni, 'lots of footprints in the mud here. The police should be along taking casts.' They sidestepped the footprints and went to the mill house, but there was no answer to May's doorbell.

'I'm hot and hungry,' said Simon. 'What if we buy some lunch and drive up out of the village and find a pleasant place for a picnic?'

'But not at the local store,' said Toni. 'I can't bear any more of their hate. You said they wouldn't attack us in daylight, but remember those kids throwing clods of earth at us.'

'School's in so we should be safe. But there's a shop at a garage out on the ring road. We'll get some stuff there.'

Armed with sandwiches and soft drinks, they drove back through the village and up to the top of a hill, where there was a bench overlooking a hay field.

The hay had been bundled up into great round bales. 'How peaceful and rural it all is,' said Toni, as a tractor made its way across the field, picking up each bale with a spear mounted at the front and heading back to the barn.

'They have to get the spear right in the middle of the bale,' said Simon. 'If it scrapes against the ground, it can foul the whole thing up. Have a salmon sandwich.'

'Thanks. Here comes the tractor again.'

The tractor chugged back. The spear was thrust into the next bale. Simon stared. Something black, which yet glinted red in the sunlight, was oozing out from the bale. He vaulted the fence, crying, 'Stop! Stop!'

The tractor driver could not hear him above the noise

of the engine but saw Simon shouting and yelling as he raced across the field.

He switched off the engine and asked truculently, 'What's up with ye?'

'There's blood coming out of that bale,' gasped Simon.

'So what? Probably a fox or rabbit or something.'

'Don't move that bale another inch. I'm calling the police.'

'I've already phoned them,' said Toni, joining him. 'Call Agatha.'

A tall man in a blue open-necked shirt and jeans strode rapidly across the field. 'Here's the boss,' said the tractor driver with gloomy relish. 'You're for it now.'

'I'm Gerald Fairfield, the farmer,' said the man. 'What's up, Andy?'

'This 'ere precious pair's screaming there's blood coming out of the bale.'

'So it's some animal or other,' said Gerald impatiently.

Toni rapidly explained about the missing journalist.

Despite his shock, Simon noticed the farmer was quite handsome. His angry face softened as he looked at Toni as she blurted out the explanation about the missing reporter.

'Well, young lady,' he said. 'We'll wait until the police get here, but I think you'll find you've just made great fools of yourselves.'

Bill Wong was the first to arrive, followed by two policemen. He studied the bale and then said, 'We've got to wait for SOCO to arrive.'

'You're surely not taking this seriously,' protested Gerald.

'Very seriously,' said Bill. 'Here come the scene-of-crime operatives. I suggest we all back off before we're accused of compromising what may be a murder scene.'

They all retreated to the edge of the field as the white-coated figures advanced with their equipment. Simon found a pair of binoculars in his car and studied the scene. The wire around the bale was cut and SOCO began their search.

Out of the hay finally tumbled a crumpled body.

Gerald and Andy were standing with Simon and Toni and the waiting police.

'Didn't you do that field the night before last, Andy?' asked Gerald.

'Yes, boss. You know that. All day yesterday as well and right on into the evening after dark, it was.'

Agatha arrived with Phil and Patrick. She handed Bill Ruby's card. 'You'd better send someone up to Hackney in London to fetch her to identify the body,' she said.

'There's still mud down by the millpond lane with a lot of footprints in it,' said Simon.

'Right,' said Wilkes. 'We'll get on to it.' He turned to Agatha. 'I want you to leave all this to us. We can't have private detectives cluttering up the scene.'

'You wouldn't be cluttering up the scene yourself,' protested Agatha, 'if my detectives hadn't found the body.'

'I want your two detectives to go back to headquarters with you, Mrs Raisin, and make statements.'

Bill whispered to Agatha, 'Call on you later.'

* * *

Agatha and her staff, with the exception of Mrs Freedman, waited anxiously that evening in her cottage for Bill to arrive. Charles had joined them, saying he had ordered steak pies to be delivered from the pub, therefore saving everyone from a selection of supermarket curries from Agatha's freezer.

Bill arrived just as they were finishing their dinner. 'It's a right mess,' he said. 'Yes, it's Dan Palmer and it's worse even than you think. The preliminary autopsy shows that he was possibly unconscious but alive when the baler scooped him up and stabbed him as a final insult. He was probably smothered to death.'

'How's Mrs Palmer taking it?'

'Pretty easily. In fact, so easily that Wilkes got a check on her, but she was definitely back in Hackney after she left you. Also, she's too small a woman to hit a man like Dan and then somehow get his body up into the hay field. They estimate the hay was still uncut when the body was dumped but that it was placed just where the baler would be bound to pick it up. Andy swears he saw nothing. We've got men going from door to door. We cannot find Palmer's car.

'There's another thing, Simon. Are you really sure you saw footprints in the mud in Mill Lane?'

'Yes.'

'Something had flattened them over. Why did you think footprints in Mill Lane were particularly interesting?'

Simon looked at Agatha. 'Oh, go on, tell him,' said Agatha.

So Simon told of the attempt on his life and how he had lied to the vicar and told him he could not swim.

'Now, listen to me carefully,' said Bill. 'We have set up a mobile unit again in the village and the place is swarming with detectives and police officers, not to mention the press. I want you all to keep clear. We don't want another dead body on our hands.

'Even out of the village, in Mircester, I want you to be careful. You found the body, so the murderer might consider life safer with one of you out of the way, probably Simon. You've got other cases, haven't you? Get on with them.'

James Lacey sat in his hotel room in Singapore and watched the latest news from Odley Cruesis on BBC TV international news. Agatha was in the thick of it, as usual, he thought. He missed her. He really had to admit that he missed her. But he dreaded the contempt in her bearlike eyes when she looked at him. He wondered if she would ever forgive him for having fallen for that airhead he had so nearly married.

After they had all left, including Charles, Agatha made herself a cup of strong black coffee and lit a cigarette. She had recently given up smoking when other people were around unless they were outside in the open air. She decided to sit up during the night and carefully read all the notes on the case of John Sunday from beginning to end. At last she struggled up to bed with a nagging feeling she had just missed something important.

In the following two weeks, Agatha and her staff diligently went about their work, Agatha trying to put the murders of John Sunday and Dan Palmer out of her mind. The police had drained the millpond in the hope of finding Dan's car, but there was no sign of it, only the remains of his listening device.

'I daren't go back to that village,' said Agatha to Mrs Bloxby one evening, 'but I would like to get another look at all of them. I know!'

'Know what?' asked the vicar's wife uneasily.

'Well, the Ladies' Society here is always hosting other villages and they host us. Why don't we invite Odley Cruesis for . . . let me think . . . a special cream tea event in the village hall here. Teas at two pounds a head, plus coaches to bring them over. Give the money to charity. Alzheimer's could do with the money.'

'Mrs Raisin! Think of the expense. We could not recoup enough to cover our own costs, let alone give anything to charity.'

'I'll pay for the lot. I will not let this murderer go free. Don't worry, I'll organize everything. Oh, and the village band to be hired to play jolly sounds.'

There was a ring at the doorbell. Mrs Bloxby went to answer it and returned with Charles. 'Oh, Charles,' said Agatha, 'I've had a great idea.'

Charles sat down on the sofa next to her and listened to her plans. 'You'd better hire a couple of portaloos as well,' he said. 'Think of all the wrinklies that'll turn up. Think of all the weak bladders and swollen prostates. As far as I remember, the hall has only the one toilet.'

'I'll fix it,' said Agatha, her eyes gleaming.

'Agatha,' said Charles plaintively, 'you haven't told me why.'

'I want to be able to sit there and *study* the lot of them.'

'And you think your feminine intuition will kick in and you'll stand up and shout "Eureka!" and point at someone. When a photo of a murderer appears in the newspapers, a lot of people say things like, "Look at the eyes! Now, there's a killer." Whereas before they were trapped, they probably looked very ordinary.'

'There must be something. Two weeks' time. I'll get the posters printed off tomorrow and send them over to the vicarage.'

'What if no one comes?' asked Charles. 'I mean, I bet they know you live here and think there might be something fishy.'

'For a cream tea at two pounds a head and free transport, they'll come.'

'Pity it's tea and not liquor,' said Charles. 'Might loosen them all up a bit.'

'There's a point,' said Agatha. 'What's that woman's name, Mrs Bloxby? The one who sells sloe gin and elderberry wine at the markets?'

'Mrs Trooly.'

'Get me her number. Good idea of yours, Charles.'

'Mrs Raisin,' said Mrs Bloxby severely, 'have you considered that an inebriated murderer might put you, for example, very much at risk?'

'All the better,' said Agatha cheerfully. 'Flush 'em out! I think there's more than one.'

Mrs Bloxby hoped it would rain on the great day, anything to stop this tea, which she considered at best a waste of money and at worst highly dangerous. But the sun shone down and the coaches bringing the visitors were all full. Agatha had hired caterers. Mrs Trooly was moving amongst the tables, offering sloe gin and wine. The band was playing old favourites and there was a general air of goodwill and jollity. Even Giles Timson smiled on Agatha. 'How very kind of you. Just what our villagers needed to take their minds off the horrors of the murders.'

Simon and Toni sat together at a table at the door. They had collected the money from the visitors and were now relaxing. 'They do seem to be enjoying themselves,' said Simon. 'Even May Dinwoody was nice to me.'

'Agatha believes in stirring things up,' said Toni. 'What are we to do with the money?'

'Count it up,' said Simon. 'Then we give it to Mrs Freedman to put in the bank and she writes out a cheque to the Alzheimer's Society.'

'We'd better start,' sighed Toni. 'Some of them must have been raiding the piggy bank to pay their two pounds.'

'Agatha thinks of everything. She's left us piles of these little plastic bags from the bank, some for pennies, some for twenty-pence pieces and so on. Let's see how quickly we can do it and then we'll go in there and sample the sloe gin, if there's any left.'

Penelope Timson brought over a chair and squeezed next to Agatha. 'This is such fun,' she said.

'Yes,' said Agatha bleakly. No one looked edgy. No one looked frightened or ill at ease. 'I'll just see how the young people are getting on.'

She went to the door, where Toni and Simon were putting coins into bags. 'Nearly finished,' said Toni cheerfully.

'I'm going outside for a smoke,' said Agatha.

She sat down on a bench outside and lit up a cigarette. Must give these wretched things up, she thought for the umpteenth time. From inside she could hear the chatter of voices rising above the noise of the band. Charles came out and joined her. He was wearing a deep-blue cotton shirt, open at the neck, and blue chinos and yet somehow looked as neat and composed as if he were in suit, collar and tie.

'Give me one of those.'

'A cigarette, Charles? Bad for you.'

'Too right. Hand one over.'

He lit it and settled back on the bench. 'Hasn't something struck you as funny?'

'No. What?'

'Look at it this way. We know they're a sour lot and Carrie Brother, for example, is hardly the flavour of the month in that village, and yet they're all wolfing down cream teas, gulping back sloe gin, and going on like a love-in.'

Agatha sat up straight. 'You mean, they're all putting on an act?'

'Looks like it to me.'

'But why? I mean, they must think there's a murderer amongst them.'

'Maybe they have a good idea who it is. *They* feel safe. Look at it from their point of view. John Sunday was an interfering pest, Dan Palmer was just asking for it, Simon was a cheat and a spy and so on. I should think every man jack of them has guessed why this sudden burst of generosity on your part and they're playing up to the hilt.'

'Well, thank goodness the proceeds are going to the Alzheimer's Society,' said Agatha gloomily. 'I may need their help soon. Should I stir things up? Should I go in there and say I know the identity of the murderer?'

'And like Roy, the same thing could happen to you. Forget it. Enjoy the day.'

'Got over Sharon?' Simon asked Toni as they finally finished bagging up and recording all the money.

'Not quite,' said Toni. 'I keep thinking I see her. I'll see someone ahead of me in the street, some girl with multicoloured hair wearing a boob tube and torn jeans, and I want to run after her. I keep wondering if I could have done anything. I shouldn't have let Agatha turn her out of my flat.'

'And then you might have been dead as well. She'd have started inviting her biker friends back to the flat. Would you like to go to a movie with me tonight?'

'Fine. Which one?'

'I don't know. I'd just thought of the idea.'

The day was finally over. Not one scone or bit of straw-berry jam or bowl of whipped cream was left. Mrs Trooly had taken away the remainder of her drinks after handing Agatha a bill. The men came to take away the portaloos and complained bitterly at the state of them. 'Some of them just peed on the floor,' complained one of the men. 'Dirty old hicks.' He was a Birmingham man and considered the countryside outside the city to be peopled with inbred imbeciles.

Agatha helped the caterers and village ladies to clean up the mess before she and Charles wearily trudged back to her cottage.

'I'm going back to study my notes,' said Agatha. 'I swear there's something there.'

'I'll be off, then,' said Charles.

Agatha suddenly did not want to be left alone. 'Charles, please . . .'

He swung round and looked at her seriously. 'Please what?'

'Nothing,' said Agatha gruffly. 'I'll see you when I see you.'

She fed her cats and let them out into the garden and then collected her folders of notes and took them out to the garden table.

Agatha began to read. She found Simon's account of his trip to Cheltenham particularly amusing, as she remembered the days when she had to ferry around a horrible old couple called Boggle. Then she suddenly put the folders down on the table. Elderly . . . toilets . . . the portaloo man's complaints.

She phoned Penelope Timson. 'Oh, Mrs Raisin. Thank you again for such a fine day.'

'I just wanted to ask you,' said Agatha. 'Do you have a downstairs toilet?'

'Yes, just as you come in the front door, on the left.'

'I must come over and see you. It's terribly important.'

'Well, really . . . All right, but I plan to go to bed early.'

In the vicarage parlour, Agatha fixed Penelope with an intense gaze and said, 'Now, you said that no one left the room during the evening John Sunday was murdered, except Miriam and Miss Simms. Right?'

'Yes, and I told the police so as well. I don't see—'

'Think! Did no one leave briefly to use the toilet?'

'Yes, but it's just outside the door.'

'Who?'

'This really is so embarrassing. I mean, one doesn't talk about such things. I was brought up to—'

'*Who?*' shouted Agatha.

'Let me see, I suppose Mr Beagle and maybe Mr Summer.'

'Right!' Agatha got to her feet and the next thing Penelope heard was the outside door slam.

Chapter Eleven

Agatha called an emergency meeting of her staff for eight o'clock the following morning.

She described what she had learned and then said, 'So you see it could either have been Charlie Beagle or Fred Summer.'

'But they're so old,' protested Toni.

'They're fit enough to put up all those Christmas decorations each year. One of them tips John Sunday off that there's going to be a meeting about him at the vicarage. He's a snoop, so he creeps up. Either Charlie or Fred nips out as if to go to the loo, gets in the garden, Grudge Sunday is moving up to the vicarage windows, so one of them stabs him and dives back into the house.'

Simon looked excited. 'Wait a bit. Whoever it was wouldn't like to be sitting around with a bloody knife, knowing the police would be called the minute the body was found.'

'Maybe the murderer didn't expect Sunday to be found until after the confab was over,' pointed out Patrick. 'Whoever it was might not have expected Sunday to stagger up to the windows and die in front of everyone.'

'Yes, but even so. Where would the murderer hide a knife?'

'In the cistern in the toilet?' suggested Phil. 'But the police must have done a thorough search for the weapon.'

'But,' said Agatha, practically jumping up and down with excitement, 'when they were assured that no one apart from Miriam and Miss Simms had left the room, they didn't search any of us. The murderer might not have depended on that. The police were searching *outside* the vicarage for a weapon.'

'So we just tell the police,' said Patrick, 'and start them off on a new search.'

'I found this out,' said Agatha stubbornly. 'And I'm going to find out the rest of it. I'll get Mrs Bloxby to go over to the vicarage with me to report on the takings from the teas. I'll go to the loo and look around and search the hall as well.'

'Who is this Miss Simms?' asked Simon. 'Are you sure she couldn't have done it?'

'Not the type. Besides, she left with Miriam and was with her the whole time.'

'You know,' said Phil uneasily, 'it was quite a time ago now. Our murderer has had plenty of opportunity to go back to the vicarage and get the knife back.'

Agatha's face fell. Then she said stubbornly, 'I'm going to try.'

'I think you should let us know the time you're going to be in the vicarage,' said Patrick, 'and we'll all park somewhere nearby so you can call us if there's any danger. Remember, the vicar left for his study and he is reputed to have a violent temper.'

'And I can't imagine two oldies murdering anyone over Christmas tree lights,' said Simon.

'I can,' said Agatha defiantly. 'Those lights were the highlight of their miserable lives.'

Agatha drove back to Carsely and told her startled friend, Mrs Bloxby, of her plan.

'But the police . . .' began the vicar's wife in protest.

'Sod the police! They'd descend in droves and clump around, alerting everybody. One of those villagers might have a nephew or a cousin in police headquarters for all we know.'

'Very well. I'll just get the record of the money we took at the teas to make it all look respectable.'

Penelope welcomed them effusively. 'Such a success! I do think good works give one a positive glow. Now, let's have a nice cup of tea in the garden. They say the weather is going to break, so this will be our last chance for a while to get some sunshine.'

Agatha waited impatiently until they were settled in their garden chairs and Penelope had brought out the tea tray, and then said, 'Do excuse me.'

'It's on the first landing, if you want to powder your nose,' said Penelope.

'Haven't you got one in the hall?'

'So dark. You'd be much better upstairs.'

'I'll be fine,' said Agatha, and made her escape.

The toilet off the hall was small and dark. It was old-fashioned with a high cistern and a long chain. There was a tiny window at the back which looked as if it had not been opened in ages. Beside the toilet was a small shelf of books of an improving nature – *Is God in Your Life?*, *Meetings with Jesus*, and so on.

Agatha carefully removed all the books but found nothing behind them. She put them back. Then the door handle of the toilet rattled. 'Who's in there?' called Giles' voice.

'Agatha Raisin. Sorry, I'm a bit constipated.'

She stood with her heart thumping until she heard him go up the stairs. Now, where else? There was a high shelf with spare toilet rolls. She stood on the seat of the lavatory pan and began to search behind them. Nothing.

She got back down and sat down wearily on top of the lavatory. Then she studied the floor. It was covered in old green linoleum, some of it warped with damp and age. She got down on her knees and began to pull up pieces of it.

Agatha could hardly believe her eyes when she finally ripped a lump clear from one corner and found herself looking down at a kitchen knife.

She pulled out her phone and called Patrick. 'I've found the weapon. Get the police!'

There came a timid knock at the door: Penelope. 'Are you all right, Mrs Raisin?'

Should she tell her? No.

'Badly constipated,' she shouted. 'Won't be long.'

'Oh, dear. I have some Seneca. If you slide open the door a crack I can slip it in with a glass of water.'

'I'll be all right,' roared Agatha.

What was keeping the police so long? Then to her horror she heard a voice she recognized as that of Fred Summer. 'What's going on?'

'Nothing, Mr Summer,' she heard Penelope say. 'Mrs Raisin is using our toilet.' Penelope raised her voice. 'All right now, Mrs Raisin?' Agatha stood up and pulled the chain and then washed her hands at the hand basin. Then she shouted, 'The door's stuck.'

'That's all right,' came Fred's voice. 'Charlie's here with his hammer.'

'I did a silly thing,' called Agatha. 'I called the police!'

'You *what*?' screeched Penelope.

'You don't want your door knocked down with a hammer. I'm sure the police have lock picks.'

Giles, the vicar, joined the group outside. Then Carrie Brother. Agatha began to feel like Alice in Wonderland when she had her foot stuck up the chimney. Then Charlie Beagle shouted, 'Stand back all. I'll 'ave 'er out!'

The heavy blow of a hammer struck the door. Then Agatha heard the wail of a police siren.

Then Bill's voice. 'Put that hammer down. Are you all right, Mrs Raisin?'

Agatha opened the door and pointed mutely to the torn linoleum and the knife. 'I haven't touched it,' she said.

'Right,' said Bill. 'Out you come. I'll seal off this door until the forensics team arrives.'

Fred Summer, Charlie Beagle and Carrie Brother had disappeared.

'Will someone please tell me what is going in my house?' demanded Giles, his high, thin, reedy voice almost cracking with outrage.

'Mrs Raisin has found what looks like the weapon that murdered John Sunday under the linoleum in your toilet,' said Bill. 'Now, Agatha, just come out into the garden and I'll take your initial statement.'

'You'd better send some police to bring in Charlie Beagle and Fred Summer,' said Agatha. 'Then I'll tell you.'

Bill barked orders. 'Wait here, Agatha. I've got to phone Wilkes.' He turned away and began talking rapidly into his mobile phone. Then he turned back to Agatha.

'Right! Let's have it.'

Agatha explained how she had guessed that perhaps one of the old people might have gone out to use the toilet and that the vicar's wife would not think it decent to say so.

'You'll need to get taken off to headquarters and make a full statement.' He signalled to a policewoman. 'Take Mrs Raisin to headquarters and get a full statement from her.'

'I'll follow you in my own car,' said Agatha.

A policeman came running back. 'Can't find them,' he gasped.

'What kind of car have they got?'

'The neighbours say they haven't got a car.'

'Off you go, Agatha. I need more men out here to check the fields.'

'Wait!' cried Agatha. 'Dan Palmer's car.' She scrabbled in her bag and brought out her notebook and flipped through the pages. 'Here it is.' She gave Bill the make and registration. 'That car was never found. They could be using that.'

Bill went back to his car and frantically radioed instructions for roadblocks to be set up.

As she drove, Agatha phoned Toni and Simon and told them to start searching for the missing Beagles and Summers.

Agatha waited impatiently at police headquarters for someone to interview her. After an hour, she was shown into the old interview room she remembered so well – scarred table, institutional green walls and hard chairs.

A woman detective Agatha had not met before came in, flanked by a police sergeant. 'I am Detective Sergeant Annie Plack and this is Police Sergeant Peter Lynn,' she began.

Annie Plack had shiny black hair and clear blue eyes. Agatha wondered vaguely if Bill had fallen for her yet.

The tape was switched on and Agatha began her statement. Annie had heard stories about Agatha, how she never did any real detective work, just blundered about and stirred things up until something had cracked. But she had to admit that no detective or police officer could have hit on the idea that the vicar's wife would consider it not genteel to mention anyone leaving to use the loo.

When Agatha had signed her statement, she was told to wait in the reception area.

At last, Annie came out and sat down next to her. 'It has been suggested that we put you up in a safe flat for the next few days. A policewoman will go to your home and wait until you pack up.'

Agatha thought of her cats. 'I'll be all right,' she said mutinously. 'I've got a burglar alarm. They're old people.'

'They may have committed two murders, Mrs Raisin, the last one being particularly nasty.'

'No, I absolutely refuse. I'll be all right.'

Simon, accompanied by Toni, decided to call on May Dinwoody. No one in the village was talking to either them or the police. Simon hoped it might still be possible that May would talk to him.

May was about to close the door in his face when Simon said urgently, 'We can pay for information.'

The door opened a few inches.

'How much?' asked May, thinking of her straitened circumstances.

'Two hundred pounds.'

'Come in, then. But what can I tell you that could possibly be worth two hundred pounds?'

'Fred and Charlie have disappeared along with their wives. They may have the car that belonged to that reporter. You know the countryside around here. Where could they possibly go that the police would not think of looking?'

May sat in silence, her brow wrinkled up in thought. Then she said, 'There's just the one place.'

'Where's that?' asked Toni.

'Thirley Grange. It belonged to Sir Mark Thirley who died last year. Terrible death duties. But it's a Georgian gem and his nephew has managed to get the National Trust to agree to take it over. They haven't started work yet, but they've put a man at the lodge and repaired the walls and fences and they've got a night watchman to patrol the place. There are a lot of outbuildings and stables and things and an old folly in the grounds.'

'Is there any way they could get in past the man at the lodge?' asked Simon.

'I used to wander round there last year before the Trust began work. It was so quiet, and the grounds, although badly in need of upkeep, are still pretty. There is a back road . . . Wait. I've got an ordnance survey map. I bought it when I first moved here so it might be out of date.'

She left the room. Simon walked to the window and looked down at the millpond. The day had turned grey and chilly and a rough breeze creased the waters. He swung round as May came back into the room. 'Here we are,' she said, spreading the map on the table. 'That is the Grange and just there, that dotted line, that's a back road. It was used in the old days by tradesmen, but I don't think it's been used since the middle of the last century. After the war, the old habits died away and people couldn't find staff and so the tradesmen just went up the main drive.'

'Why do you think they did it?' asked Toni.

'*If* they did,' said May severely. 'Oh, dear, it was those

207

Christmas lights. They were photographed in *Cotswold Life* and then they were filmed on Midlands TV. They were so proud. Then John Sunday turned up to ruin it all. Money, please.'

Simon took out his chequebook, and wrote out a cheque for two hundred pounds.

May blushed. 'I shouldn't be taking this, but times are hard.'

'We'll just borrow this map,' said Simon, 'and I'll return it to you later.'

Outside, they tried to phone Agatha, but she was being interviewed and had her phone switched off.

'We'll go and recce anyway,' said Simon. 'We'll take your car. My motorbike makes too much noise.'

Thirley Grange was buried in a fold of the Cotswold hills a good fifteen miles from the village. There were no signposts to it.

They finally located a weedy lane beside the ruin of a cottage. 'Look!' exclaimed Toni. 'I think someone's been through here already. You can just make out car tracks. Oh, Simon, we really should phone the police.'

'And they'll arrive with sirens blaring and helicopters overhead and we may never catch them,' said Simon. 'We'd look like real amateurs. See how far along you can drive.'

Toni set off again. Trees and bushes began to press against the car on either side. She finally stopped again.

'I'm not going to sacrifice my paintwork on a hunch,' she said. 'Let's get out and walk.'

'It can't be that far,' said Simon as they trudged along. 'I mean, May said it was a Georgian gem. Gems surely don't have that much land.'

They walked forward under the green shade of the overarching trees. Simon suddenly stopped. A patch of mud on the road showed clear tyre tracks.

Toni took out her phone. 'I'm trying Agatha again.'

'Why?'

'Because she's the boss. You don't keep things like this away from Agatha.'

This time Toni got Agatha and talked rapidly. 'Don't run into danger. You catch a glimpse of even one of them, call the police. I'm coming.'

Agatha phoned Charles. 'Toni thinks they might be hiding out at a place called Thirley Grange. Know it? They're on a back road to it.'

'Where are you?'

'Parked in front of police headquarters.'

'I'm in Mircester. I'll be with you in a minute.'

Agatha thought she ought to call Patrick and Phil off the jobs they were working on, but then decided against it. It was too much of a long shot that they would find the couples.

Charles joined her and they set off.

'There's the back of the house,' whispered Toni as they emerged from the trees sheltering the road. 'What should we do now?'

'I think we should hide back in the trees and bushes and watch,' said Simon.

They crouched down in the bushes and waited. The house seemed ruined, empty and deserted. 'If they drove right up,' whispered Toni, 'then their car must be badly scratched. I noticed an awful lot of broken twigs and branches as we walked along. They must be there. No one else would be crazy enough to force a car along that road.'

'Agatha won't be long now,' whispered Simon. 'You should have left it to us.'

Toni took her mobile out again. 'I'm phoning the police.'

'You're *what*?' Simon made a grab for her phone, but Toni darted away from him and into the trees. She had felt a sudden frisson of fear. It was almost as if her old friend Sharon was around, telling her not to be such a fool. Toni still had Bill Wong's mobile phone number programmed in her phone from the days when they used to date. She called it. 'Bill, I'm at Thirley Grange. I think they're here. I'm—'

A low voice in her ear said, 'If you wants to see your boyfriend again, missy, drop that phone.'

Toni swung round. Fred Summer stood there, holding a hunting knife. 'Drop it!' he snarled. Toni dropped the phone and Fred ground it under foot. 'Now, march!'

Toni was urged forward, feeling the point of that knife at her back. Simon was where she had left him, but he was lying face down on the ground and Charlie Beagle was standing over him, holding a shotgun.

'On yer feet,' said Charlie. 'Both of you into the house.'

Bill Wong called for urgent reinforcements. Then he called Agatha. 'What were you doing sending that young pair into danger? They've been caught. Don't go any further if you're on your way there. Two people are enough to rescue.'

'What was that about?' asked Charles, who was driving. Agatha told him. Charles pressed harder on the accelerator and the car leapt forward. 'We'll go in by the main gate,' he said. 'We could waste valuable time looking for that side road.'

A man came hurrying out of the lodge house and held up a hand. Charles lowered the window and shouted to him that escaped murderers were hiding up at the Grange. The lodge keeper dashed to open the gates. 'Have you any guns?' called Charles.

'Couple of shotguns and a rifle.'

'Bring them quick and get in the car.'

Agatha fretted with impatience. Was Toni alive? How could she ever forgive herself if something had happened to the girl?

Toni and Simon were forced down into a cellar. They heard the door above being locked and then they were alone. A faint light shone from a cobwebbed window up near the ceiling.

'They're going to kill us,' said Toni. 'They're up there right now figuring out how to dispose of us.'

'What happened? Did Fred hear you calling the police?'

'Yes.'

'Then with any luck they're going to make their escape and leave us locked up here. I wish we could find some way out. They are murderers, after all.'

'Turn your back,' said Toni, feeling her way off into a dark corner.

'Why?'

'I've got to pee. I nearly peed myself out there.'

When she rejoined him, she said, 'That's coal over there, isn't it?'

'Yes. What are you planning? To throw lumps at them when they come back?'

'Coal means a coal hole, see? That's how the coal got down here. It's not a wine cellar. It's where they kept the coal.'

'Right,' said Simon eagerly. 'It must be up there somewhere.'

Charles drove up to the front door. The lodge keeper, who had introduced himself as Matt Fox, jumped out and unlocked the front door.

'Wait!' shouted Agatha. 'I can hear a car.'

'It's coming from the back,' said Charles. Matt jumped back in the car as Charles drove round to the back of the building.

'That's Dan Palmer's car,' shouted Agatha. 'They're not taking the side road. They're circling round to go down the main drive.' Matt was hurriedly loading a rifle in the backseat. They sped after them at a frantic pace. Matt lowered the window, leaned out and took careful aim. He shot out one back tyre and then the other. Then just as the Volvo reached the lodge gates, Matt shot out its back window with one of the shotguns.

The Volvo screeched and swayed across the road, straight into the path of a huge articulated lorry. There was a sickening *crump* – and then silence.

'Agatha, go and see if that lorry driver is all right. Matt, give me a shotgun. Is it loaded?'

'Yes.'

Charles shot in the window of his own car. 'Self-defence, see?' he said.

Agatha was helping the lorry driver out of his cab as two police cars came racing up. Bill came out of the first one. 'I've got to get back to the Grange,' she howled. 'They've taken Toni and Simon.'

'Just wait there. We'll handle it.'

Police were taping off the road. A van full of scene-of-crime operatives stopped, climbed out and began to put on their white suits and masks. Inspector Wilkes arrived. 'Now, what happened?' he asked grimly.

'Are they dead?' asked Agatha.

Wilkes looked at the crumpled wreck of the Volvo. 'Yes. Now, begin at the beginning. You first, Mrs Raisin.'

Agatha was about to speak when a car drove out past the lodge and stopped. Toni and Simon, black with coal dust, got out and stood staring at the scene of carnage.

213

Agatha Raisin ran straight to Toni and flung her arms around her. 'Oh, I'm so glad you're alive.'

It was a long day. Statements, statements and more statements. Then Agatha, Charles and Toni, along with the lodge keeper, were taken back to police headquarters for further grilling.

They learned that the Grange had been searched and there was no sign of either Mrs Summer or Mrs Beagle. Matt backed the story of self-defence and Agatha insisted it was put down in her statement that the lodge keeper was a hero.

By early evening, Wilkes went out to face the press and make a brief statement.

At last, Agatha and the rest were told they were free to go home.

In the weeks that followed, it transpired that Charlie and Fred had sold their cottages to a builder two months before their deaths. Their bank accounts had been cleared out a week before their flight. Fred's finger-prints had been found on the knife that Agatha had found at the vicarage along with DNA evidence that the blood on the knife belonged to the late, unlamented John Sunday.

A massive search for the missing wives was put into operation, but they seemed to have disappeared into thin air.

214

'How can two such frail elderly ladies escape the police just like that?' Agatha exclaimed one evening to her friend, Mrs Bloxby.

'Perhaps easier than you think,' said Mrs Bloxby. 'No one notices the elderly. Buses run along that road going to Cheltenham.'

'But surely the police have questioned all the bus drivers?'

'I'm sure one elderly lady looks much like another to these men. Did they have passports?'

'Yes, fairly new ones, too. And it's not as if they would know anyone who could get them fake ones.'

'Perhaps I might be able to do it,' said Mrs Bloxby dreamily. 'I'd head for some seaside resort where there are a lot of elderly people and set about stealing a few from handbags. It wouldn't be handbag snatching. Maybe a seat in a shelter looking at the sea. Friendly talk. Visit to the public toilets. More talk while hands are washed. Handbags are often left at the basin while women go to dry their hands. Quick dip and out comes a passport. Now, if you're an elderly lady and you have still got your money and keys, you might not notice your passport is missing for some time. Even if you go to the police, to them you're just another forgetful old woman.'

'Really, Mrs Bloxby. You would make a very good criminal. Toni and Simon have searched and searched.'

'They make a nice pair. Do you think they'll get engaged?' asked Mrs Bloxby.

Agatha stiffened. 'They're too young! They're just colleagues.'

'Ah, propinquity, Mrs Raisin.'

'It won't do,' said Agatha. 'They are two very good detectives and I don't want Toni off having babies when she's little more than a baby herself.'

'But, Mrs Raisin,' said the vicar's wife with a steely note in her voice, 'you would not possibly do anything to spoil a budding romance?'

'Me? Perish the thought,' said Agatha, and crossed her fingers behind her back.

Bill Wong was waiting for Agatha after she left the vicarage and returned to her home. 'Social call?' asked Agatha.

'Sort of. Been visiting Mrs Bloxby?'

'Yes, she came up with some interesting ideas. Do you want me to get rid of the cats? They're crawling all over you.'

'No, I like them.' Hodge was draped around Bill's neck and Boswell had jumped up into his arms. 'But maybe I'll put them in the garden if you've got anything very interesting.'

'Might be.'

Bill opened the garden door and detached the cats.

'Now,' he said, sitting down at the kitchen table. 'What gives?'

Agatha told him of Mrs Bloxby's theories.

'Unfortunately, she may be right. Can you imagine all that murder and mayhem over Christmas lights?'

'I can in a way. Some of these people on reality TV

have their moment of fame and never get over it. John Sunday was a thoroughly nasty man and must have enjoyed thwarting them. You know the bus drivers on that route past the Grange. How were they interviewed?'

'Back at the depot.'

'Did you have photographs of the two women?'

'Yes, we got a photo from *Cotswold Life*. There's really only the one driver that does that route.'

'I'd like to start at the beginning of their journey. In the meantime, do you think your boss would let you phone up watering holes around the south coast to see if any elderly women reported missing passports a few days after Mrs Summers and Mrs Beagle disappeared?'

'I'll probably need to do it in my own time.'

'I'll get Patrick on to it as well. They would be gussied up for their photo in *Cotswold Life*. I think I might trot over to that hellish village and see if I can get a better one.'

Penelope Timson gave Agatha a cautious welcome. 'I am so glad it is all over,' she said. 'I do hope you haven't come about some other murder.'

'No, no,' said Agatha soothingly. 'Nothing like that. Have you any photographs of Mrs Summer and Mrs Beagle?'

'The police got a very good one from *Cotswold Life*.'

'Yes, but I need more informal ones.'

'Oh, I might have something. I found a box of photos

taken at village fêtes. But you should have some yourself, Mrs Raisin. Wasn't someone taking photographs at that cream tea?'

'Of course. Phil. Thanks.'

Agatha phoned Phil and said she would meet him at his cottage in Carsely, where she knew he had a dark room and kept neat files of photographs.

She waited impatiently as he went searching for the photographs of the tea party. At last he came back and handed her a photo. 'There you are.'

'Genius!' said Agatha. It was a clear shot of Mrs Beagle and Mrs Summer, sitting together. 'What are their first names? I can never remember.'

'On the back of the photo: Gladys Summer and Dora Beagle.'

'Grand.'

'Starting again?'

'You bet.'

Toni waited at the depot in Cheltenham for the bus to come in. When it arrived, she waited for the passengers to dismount and then climbed on board.

'Don't leave for another half an hour, gorgeous,' said the driver, eyeing her appreciatively. 'Fancy a cup of tea?'

'All right. I just want to ask you a few questions.'

'What?'

'I'm a private detective.'

'Go on with you, lass. You're too young.'

Toni handed him her card. 'Well, I never!' he exclaimed. 'Come along then. Must have a cuppa.'

Installed in the canteen over milky cups of tea, Toni showed him the photograph. 'I know the police have asked you before, but on the day of that crash between the car and the truck, just before it, did two women like this get on your bus? This is a better photograph of them.'

He studied it carefully. 'Sorry, lass. I'd like to help you, but I'm sure they never got on.'

'Do you notice the passengers much?'

'Only if they're as pretty as you. Of course, if they're in them Muslim getups, you wouldn't know what they'd look like anyway.'

'Burkas?'

'Is that what they call 'em? Suppose so.'

Toni took a deep breath. 'Think carefully. Did two women in burkas, you know, veiled and everything, get on your bus that day?'

'As a matter of fact they did.'

'What height?'

'Pretty small. Couldn't tell you much else.'

'Where did they get off?'

'At the railway station.'

'Thanks,' said Toni.

When Toni told Agatha what she had found out, Agatha said, 'Maybe they got straight on to Eurostar and over to Brussels or Paris before the passport control at St Pancras got alerted. Nobody is going to hassle a couple of what look like Muslim women in case they're accused of racism. Snakes and bastards! They could be anywhere now.'

Chapter Twelve

Christmas was fast approaching. The piles of paperwork associated with the murders of John Sunday and Dan Palmer had at last been completed.

Bill Wong called on Agatha one evening to say that he thought the work would never be finished. The lodge keeper had had to be cleared of carrying loaded weapons and causing the crash by shooting out the wheels of the escaping car. The fact that Agatha had brought all her old public relations skills to bear on making the lodge keeper a hero had helped considerably.

'What are you doing for Christmas this year?' he asked.

'Nothing,' said Agatha firmly. 'Except I might invite Roy. Thank goodness he made a full recovery. So the case is over? What about the loose ends of Mrs Beagle and Mrs Summer?'

'Interpol are still looking for them. But no news. You know, Agatha, I don't think we'll ever find them now.'

James Lacey drove along the Mediterranean coast from Marseilles. He stopped off in the village of St

Charles-sur-Clore near Agde for the night. There seemed to be a small English expatriate community in residence. He was tired of travelling, so he booked into a small hotel called the St Charles for the night. The receptionist told him that the English residents were finding life hard because of the weak pound. Some of them were thinking of selling up and going back home. 'They used to hold their annual Christmas party here at the hotel,' she said, 'but this year they say they can't afford it.'

He went up to his room and unpacked a few essentials for the night and then went down to the bar. There were a few English couples propping up the bar, drinking glasses of the house wine and complaining about the price of everything. He ordered a whisky and took it over to a quiet corner and began to read a book on Roman military fortifications.

After a few moments, he realized the voices at the bar were becoming enraged over something other than the weak pound. 'It's not only a shameful waste of electricity,' said a thin blonde with a fake-bake face, 'it's vulgar. Lets the side down. I mean, whatever one thinks of the French, they do have *taste*.'

'Fairy lights everywhere,' said her companion, a florid man in blazer and flannels, 'even in the bushes in their garden. And they got Duval, the handyman, to put that Santa on the chimney. And they're old. It's not as if they have any grandchildren.'

James slowly put down his book. He had followed the murder of John Sunday in the newspapers and television. He got up and went to the bar. 'May I buy a round?' he asked.

Faces beamed at him. Drinks were rapidly changed from wine to spirits. 'I couldn't help overhearing what you were saying,' said James. 'Someone going a bit over the top?'

'It's an elderly couple of ladies just outside the village,' said the florid man. 'They've got lights all over the place like one of those awful Americans.'

'Sounds fun. I'd like to have a look,' said James. 'How do I get there? Should I drive?'

'Don't really need to. Turn left as you go out of the hotel door and keep on going about half a mile. You can't miss it. Their stupid cottage lights up the sky.'

James went out into the evening. It was quite mild and clear with a small moon riding high above the twisted chimneys of the old houses in the village. As he passed the last house in the village, he saw a glow in the sky ahead of him and quickened his step. At last he came to the cottage. There were so many Christmas decorations, it was an exercise in vulgarity. A spotlight had even been placed in the garden to highlight a leering Santa clinging to the chimney.

He marched up the path and knocked on the door. 'Who are you?' shouted a voice from an upstairs window.

James stood back and looked up. He could just make out an elderly woman half hidden behind a curtain.

'I've just been admiring your lights,' he said.

'Go away,' croaked the woman. 'Shove off.'

James walked thoughtfully back to his hotel.

The wives of the murderers were missing. They had been famous for their display of Christmas lights. Their pride in that display had led to the murders. Could he, by some mad coincidence, have found them?

He joined the English at the bar and, to their delight, paid for another round. 'When did the two old ladies arrive here?' he asked.

The florid man introduced himself as Archie Frank and his wife as Fiona. The others supplied names but James immediately forgot all of them – he was concentrating so hard on finding out about the occupants of the cottage. 'Came about two months ago,' said Archie. 'We don't see them. They get a local girl to do their shopping. Keep themselves to themselves.'

James made some small talk and then escaped to his room. He phoned Agatha and told her about the mysterious pair and their lights.

'I'm coming over,' said Agatha. 'I'll bring a photo with me.'

'Don't come all this way for what might be nothing. Send me over the photo on my computer.'

'I'm coming!' shouted Agatha. 'I'll bring Toni. Book us rooms. What's the name of the place and directions?'

Agatha collected Toni from Mircester and drove to Birmingham airport, where they got seats on a flight to Paris. Then they took a plane to Marseilles and hired a car. With Toni driving, they set off along the coast to the village of St Charles-sur-Clore.

James was waiting for them outside. 'You shouldn't have bothered,' he said, looking at their exhausted faces.

'I must be in at the kill,' said Agatha. 'I've got a good photograph of them.'

'The best way to go about it,' said James, 'is to find out the name of the village girl who does their shopping and show her the photograph. We'll check at the local store. Don't you want to dump your bags and freshen up?'

'Just for a few minutes, then,' said Agatha.

In the local grocery store, James, in his fluent French, asked the owner if he knew the identity of the girl who delivered groceries to the two old ladies in the cottage with the Christmas lights.

'That's my niece,' he said. 'Michelle!' he shouted.

A thin, small teenager with wispy hair came out of the back shop. James held out the photograph of Mrs Beagle and Mrs Summer. 'Do you deliver groceries to either of these ladies?'

'No,' she said.

'You have never seen them before?'

'No.'

'You are very sure?'

'Uncle, they are calling me a liar!'

'Get out of here,' said her uncle. 'Dirty English.'

'What was that all about?' asked Agatha outside.

'The girl says she has never seen them and told her uncle I was calling her a liar. He told me to get out. Sorry, it looks as if you've come all this way for nothing.'

'She looked shifty,' said Toni. 'I've studied that photograph for so long, I would recognize them anywhere. What if I go out there after dark on my own and watch? Look, if you didn't want anyone to know where you were and got a girl like that to shop for you, you'd probably pay her not to answer questions.'

'It's worth a try,' said Agatha wearily. 'I am so tired. I could do with a nap.'

That evening, they met up in the bar. James waved to the English propping up the bar, but shook his head when they urged him to join them.

'I'm off,' said Toni. 'I'll phone you if I get anything.'

She was wearing a black sweater and black jeans. She pulled a black wool hat over her hair and strode out along the road.

She nearly missed the cottage because all the lights had been switched off. Only a bright moon was riding high above to show her the Santa clinging to the chimney.

There was a garage at the side of the house. As she watched, an elderly figure opened the doors and climbed into a car. Toni took out a torch and shone it straight at the woman. It was Mrs Beagle. The car shot forward, nearly knocking her over, and sped off down the road.

Toni called Agatha and shouted, 'It's them! They're in the car – they're escaping. Come and pick me up.'

In what seemed like no time at all, James came racing

up in his car with Agatha beside him. 'Which way?' he shouted as Toni jumped into the backseat.

'Left.'

'That's the Agde road. Hang on.'

James put his foot down and began to drive at a hectic speed, screeching round bends, whizzing over the cobbles of silent villages, on towards Agde. 'What kind of car, Toni?'

'A red Peugeot. I didn't get the number plate.'

'There's one ahead in front of that truck.' James passed the truck. The Peugeot in front of them accelerated into Agde and headed straight for the very long jetty, which thrust its way out into the sea.

The Peugeot went straight along at breakneck speed and in front of their horrified eyes, as James stamped on the brakes, the fleeing car went straight off the end of the jetty and into the sea.

'They did a Thelma and Louise,' said Toni in a horrified voice, 'and all over a bunch of stupid Christmas lights.'

People came running out from the town, headed by two gendarmes. 'And now,' said James, 'the questioning begins.'

They were all locked up in the cells for the night and then the next day questioned over and over again, having been accused of reckless driving, terrifying two old ladies and causing their deaths. At last James persuaded a gendarme to get in touch with Interpol.

Then detectives arrived from Marseilles and the questioning began again.

Finally they were allowed to return to their hotel. Agatha took a pocket mirror out of her handbag and stared at the ruin of her face in dismay. Bags were sagging under tired, red-rimmed eyes and two little hairs had sprouted on her upper lip.

She glanced sideways at James. He looked as handsome as ever with his blue eyes in his tanned face and his thick dark hair showing only a little grey at the sides.

Why was it, she wondered bitterly, that a woman in her fifties had to start the long, long battle against loss of looks and a spreading waistline while men, provided they didn't develop a gut, could age graciously?

Toni looked tired as well, but in a graceful waif-like way.

Agatha opened her handbag and applied lipstick just as the car began to bump over the cobbles of the street leading to the hotel, and put a red smudge up under her nose.

The press were waiting outside the hotel, cameras at the ready. 'Drive on!' shouted Agatha.

James obeyed her and said, 'What's happened?'

'I've smeared my face with lipstick. Find someplace where I can repair my make-up.'

'Agatha, don't be silly. We're all exhausted and—'

'Do as she says!' Toni leapt to Agatha's defence.

James drove up a farm track and waited in angry silence while Agatha cleansed her face with moist tissues and then carefully applied foundation cream, lipstick and eyeliner.

Back at the hotel, they posed briefly for photographs before escaping indoors.

In England, three people were having different reactions to Agatha's adventures in France. Simon was wistful. He would have loved to have been there with Toni. Roy Silver felt obscurely that Agatha might have let him in on the adventure. What publicity! Charles Fraith was thoughtful.

He found himself thinking a lot about Agatha. He had taken a pretty girl out to dinner the evening before and had found himself bored with her conversation.

Now, Agatha was never boring – infuriating, rude, pushy, but never boring.

He ambled into the drawing room where his faded aunt was knitting a sweater in a violent shade of purple.

Charles sat down next to her. 'Do you remember Agatha Raisin?'

'Hard to forget her,' said his aunt. 'Never out of the newspapers.'

'What would you think about her coming to live here?'

'Good gracious, Charles. Wasn't that last marriage enough for you? Beside, she's old and can't have children.'

'I was just thinking of asking her to live here to see how it goes,' said Charles.

'Just so long as she doesn't interfere with the running of things,' said his aunt. 'But will she *fit*? I mean with your friends? And what will Gustav say?'

Gustav was Charles' gentleman's gentleman, a sort of truculent Swiss Jeeves.

'Gustav will just have to find a way of getting on with it.'

Gustav, listening outside the door, was already thinking of several ways of ousting Agatha. He had always disliked her. Gustav was a snob. He thought the word 'common' was too mild a word to describe such as Agatha Raisin.

Had Agatha come straight back from France, Charles might have dropped the idea, but the French judiciary moves in a slow and ponderous way and all he could remember as the weeks passed was what fun and adventures they had enjoyed.

He phoned Agatha from time to time, but her phone was always switched off and the hotel said that Mrs Raisin and Mr Lacey and Miss Gilmour were not taking calls. Agatha had driven into Marseilles and bought herself a new mobile phone with which she kept in communication with the office. Somehow the press had got hold of her old mobile phone number. Agatha had never thought the day would come when she would flee from publicity, until a series of photographs magnifying every wrinkle had made her feel she could not bear another interview. Then she had come down with swine flu, which meant the whole hotel was quarantined while Agatha lay in bed in her hotel room and wondered if she was going to die.

At last interest in the case died away, Agatha recovered and they were told they could go home. To her dismay, James said he would carry on through France, writing up bits and pieces for his travel books.

Just before she had been struck down with swine flu, Agatha had felt that she and James were getting on a close footing, and although she lectured herself about how useless it was to go back to the old obsession, she could almost feel it closing in on her. Then she fell ill and all she heard from James were occasional shouts from outside her bedroom door asking if she was feeling better.

Agatha found her parking fees at Birmingham airport were incredibly steep. She paid up, muttering curses under her breath, and then drove first to Mircester, where she dropped Toni off, and then set out for Carsely.

So much for global warming, thought Agatha, as fine snow began to fall, dancing hypnotically in front of the windscreen, as she drove down into Carsely.

With a sigh of relief, she let herself into her cottage. No cats. Of course, they were at her cleaner's home. She went upstairs and unpacked and changed into a loose housedress before going downstairs to make a pot of coffee.

She lit up a cigarette and coughed and gagged. I must give up, she thought. The dreaded cough. I always swore if I got a cough I would stop. But she smoked the cigarette anyway and drank a strong cup of black coffee.

The doorbell rang. Agatha went to the door and called out, 'Who is it?'

'Mrs Bloxby.'

Agatha flung open the door. 'I am so glad to see you.'

'The bush telegraph told me you had been sighted returning home, so I decided to bring you a casserole for your supper. All you have to do is heat it in the oven.'

'Come in. How good of you!'

'What adventures you have been having,' said the vicar's wife. 'And how very strange that so much murder and distress should have been caused by Christmas lights. Giles Timson did a very powerful service at Christmas, lecturing the villagers of Odley Cruesis on worldly things and how it was a spiritual festival. Then he said that Santa Claus did not exist and the villagers were furious and the newspapers called him a villain for destroying the dreams of children. Mrs Timson has left him.'

'Really? Why?'

'Her car broke down outside Mircester just after you left. She called the nearest garage and while she was waiting for the repairs, she got talking to a man called Joe Purrock, the garage owner. Evidently they hit it off right away. He is a widower. I believe Mrs Timson's appearance has quite changed. She has blonde hair now and a permanent tan and wears really ankle-breaking stilettos but she seems very happy. They went to the Maldives for Christmas. Poor you, I don't suppose you had much of a Christmas.'

'Santa came down the chimney and presented me with swine flu.'

'What did Mr Lacey give you for Christmas?'

'Sod all.'

'Peculiar man. What did you give him?'

'Well, nothing either. I lost Christmas somehow, somewhere. It all seems like a blur. I'll never forget the sight of Mrs Summer and Mrs Beagle driving straight off into the sea. If James hadn't happened to visit that village, they'd probably never have been found out.'

'I think they might. Sooner or later a local paper was going to take a picture of their cottage and some sharp Interpol man would have turned up to investigate. I mean, the murders made headlines around the world just because they were committed to stopping John Sunday from preventing them from decorating their cottages. So *odd*, you see. It made the practice quite unfashionable last Christmas, people being frightened they might be thought of as weird if they overdecorated.'

'Sherry?'

'Yes, please.'

'I'll have a G and T myself,' said Agatha. She returned with the drinks.

'Sir Charles phoned me quite a lot to see if I had heard from you,' said Mrs Bloxby.

'Probably would have liked to be in at the kill.'

Charles had decided to fetch one of his late grandmother's rings out of the bank to present to Agatha. Just to show he was, well, not exactly proposing but sort of serious before he suggested she come and live with him.

Gustav came into the study while Charles was admiring the sapphire and diamond ring. 'Who's that for?' demanded Gustav.

'Mind your own business and get me a whisky and soda.'

Gustav began to plan. His father had been a maker of clocks and musical boxes as well as being a jeweller. Gustav had worked for him, but when his father died, he had sold up the business and drifted abroad, ending up as a general factotum to Charles. He liked his life. He had full control of the running of the house. He had previously escaped from two disastrous marriages and disliked women in general and Agatha Raisin in particular.

He spent all his spare hours on his scheme. Charles phoned Mrs Bloxby and learned to his surprise that Agatha had been back for a week. He phoned her up at her office and invited her out to dinner at the George that evening.

'Who's paying?' asked Agatha suspiciously.

'I am, my sweet. Want to hear all about your adventures.'

'Bit tired of talking about them. Okay, I'll see you there. What time?'

'Eight o'clock.'

As he waited in the dining room, Charles felt quite nervous. But he relaxed as Agatha breezed in, saying, 'I'm starving. Good heavens, champagne on ice! What's the celebration?'

'You being back.'

'How sweet.'

But Agatha wondered if Charles was going to find some excuse to leave her holding the bill.

Agatha talked during the meal about her adventures. When she had finished, Charles asked, 'What do you feel for James now?'

'I don't know,' said Agatha candidly. 'I didn't spend much time with him. Same old James, if you know what I mean.'

The coffee was served.

Charles felt in his pocket and took out a red Morocco-leather box. 'Present for you.'

'Oh, Charles.'

Agatha beamed. The other diners were twisting around in their chairs.

'Open it!' urged Charles.

Agatha raised the lid. A little pig's face mounted on a coiled gold wire popped up and a tinny mechanical voice said, 'Ugly bitch! Ugly bitch!'

Agatha threw her coffee straight into Charles' face and fled the dining room, the laughter of the diners ringing in her ears.

Driving straight to Carsely, blinking her eyes to try to stop the tears running, Agatha went straight to the vicarage. Alf, the vicar, answered the door. 'Really, Mrs Raisin, we were just about to go to bed.'

'What is it?' Mrs Bloxby appeared behind him. 'Get out of the way, Alf,' she snapped. 'Can't you see she's in distress?'

The vicar stomped off and Mrs Bloxby gently led Agatha into the sitting room and settled her on the sofa.

She sat down next to her and put an arm around her shoulders as Agatha began to cry in earnest.

When Agatha had finally recovered, she told Mrs Bloxby about her dinner with Charles and about the awful pig's face and the laughter of the diners.

'No, no, *no!*' said Mrs Bloxby firmly. 'That is not like Sir Charles at all. Let me think. Maybe he meant to give you a ring. Gustav!'

'What about Gustav?'

'At one of those fêtes at Sir Charles' home, I once talked to Gustav. He told me all about being brought up in the jewellery trade. You must phone Charles.'

'No, I damn well won't.'

'Then I'll phone him. If you do not have any trust in Sir Charles, then I do.'

Mrs Bloxby went into the study and shut the door.

'It was Gustav,' said Charles bitterly. 'I was going to give Agatha my grandmother's ring and ask her to move in with me.'

'You mean, marriage?'

'That would be going a bit far. I just thought it might be rather jolly. I've fired Gustav.'

Mrs Bloxby sighed. 'Hire him back. You are not thinking straight. You think you run your estates, but Gustav does practically everything. He's irreplaceable. Can you imagine Mrs Raisin with a busy career trying to organize hunt dinners and shooting parties? What came over you? Are you in love with her?'

'I don't know. I've never been in love with anyone. What am I going to do?'

'I'll send Mrs Raisin home now. Get over to Carsely immediately and give her the real ring. Just say it was for her Christmas.'

Mrs Bloxby went back to join Agatha. 'Go home now, Mrs Raisin. Gustav played a terrible trick on Sir Charles. He wanted to give you his grandmother's ring.'

'You mean, he wants to *marry* me?'

'No, just a present.'

'I'll kill that Gustav.'

'Not tonight. Just go home.'

Agatha found Toni waiting for her outside her cottage. 'I've been searching for you,' said Toni. 'A friend's mother was at the George this evening and said a man gave you a sort of horrible jack-in-the-box ring which shouted, "Ugly bitch."'

'That was Gustav playing a trick on Charles. Come in. He's on his way over, but as it isn't an engagement, just a present, you can wait and see the real ring.'

'I always thought that Gustav was weird. He's rude. I don't know why Charles keeps him on.'

'He runs the place and Charles is lazy.' Agatha heard a car door slam outside.

'That's Charles now.'

'You sure you don't want me to leave?'

'No point. It's not as if you're interrupting a romance.'

Charles let himself in.

'What a mess,' he said wearily. 'I'm so sorry. You had such an awful time at Christmas, I wanted to give you something. Gustav knew I'd got the ring out of the bank and thought I was going to ask you to marry me.'

'And what could be more horrible than that?' said Agatha bitterly.

'Come on, Aggie. Take the bloody thing.'

Agatha suddenly smiled. 'On one condition.'

'What's that?'

'You get down on your knees and swear undying love.'

Charles laughed. 'Anything you say.'

James Lacey drove down into Carsely. He saw the lights on in Agatha's cottage. In an odd kind of way it had been exciting working with her again. He would just pop in to say goodnight and ask her out for dinner for the following evening.

The doorbell rang. 'I'll get it,' said Toni.

'It's probably Mrs Bloxby,' said Agatha. 'Now, Charles, down on your knees.'

James Lacey stood at the kitchen door. Charles was on his knees in front of Agatha. He took out a box, opened it up and held up a glittering ring. 'Be mine, my beloved. I swear undying love.'

'Oh, Charles. This is so sudden,' said Agatha.

They both heard the front door slam so loudly it seemed as if the whole cottage shook.

'Who on earth was that?' asked Charles, getting to his feet.

'James Lacey,' said Toni.

238

'I'll nip next door and explain things to him,' said Charles.

Agatha thought of James nearly marrying that stupid girl and all because she was beautiful. She remembered the pain and distress.

She caught Charles by the sleeve. 'Don't go. Don't tell him anything.'

'Like that, is it?' asked Charles.

'Yes, indeed. *Very* like that.'

Epilogue

Simon was being kept very busy by Agatha. Sometimes he felt she was keeping him *too* busy. Twice when he had bought tickets for himself and Toni to go to the theatre, Agatha had sent him out on divorce cases where he had to trail suspected adulterers for a good part of each evening.

One week, when Toni had taken a short holiday to visit her mother in Southampton, Simon found that his workload had suddenly lightened considerably, for, up until that point, Agatha had found work for him at the weekends as well.

He decided to visit May Dinwoody. He liked her and knew she found it hard to make ends meet.

She actually welcomed him, particularly as he had brought her a present of a large carton of groceries and two bottles of wine.

'So generous and thank you,' said May.

'Have you forgiven me for being a snoop?' asked Simon.

'Oh, yes. If it hadn't been for Mrs Raisin's detective agency, we really would have begun to suspect each other.'

'Are you sure nobody in the village suspected them?'

'Well, of course, people do say that they *knew*.'

'So why didn't they go to the police?'

'I think they're being wise after the event. Who in this nice village would protect murderers?'

The lot of them, possibly, thought Simon. Instead he asked, 'How are you getting on?'

Her eyes filled with tears. 'I'm going to have to sell my nice flat. I make so little from selling my toys and I can no longer make ends meet.'

'I never really looked at your toys properly,' said Simon. 'May I have a look at them?'

'If you like. Come through to my studio.'

Simon followed her and began to turn the toys over in his long fingers. They were beautifully made.

'The dolls are all made from natural stuff,' she said. 'The heads are of wood and the clothes are all handmade and from natural materials.'

'They are all very beautiful,' commented Simon.

'But the supermarkets sell such cheap plastic things. I can't compete.'

Simon stared down at the toys. Agatha Raisin had been a public relations supremo. He wondered if she could do anything.

'I've just had an idea,' he said. 'I don't want to get your hopes up. I'll call you later.'

Agatha opened the door to Simon and said, 'Come in.' The sight of him made her feel guilty. She knew she had been doing everything she could to halt his budding romance with Toni.

'Anything up?' she asked. 'Or is this just a social call?'

In the kitchen, they sat down at the table while Simon told her about May Dinwoody, ending with, 'As a former public relations guru, I thought you could think of something.'

Agatha studied him for so long that he began to feel uneasy.

At last she said, 'Yes, I could make her a success. I could lease her a shop and start a publicity campaign, but I need something from you in return.'

'What's that?'

'Toni is very young. So are you. I don't want my best detective to go off and get married and have children at her early age.'

Simon turned scarlet. 'You have no right to interfere.'

'I am determined to protect my agency. In three years' time, you can have my go ahead. Up until then, I want you to steer clear. Are you in love with her?'

'No, but almost.'

'Then it is simple. Put the brakes on and May Dinwoody can look forward to a prosperous old age.'

Simon thought of May's tear-filled eyes. Then he shrugged. 'Okay, but only until the three years are up.'

The launch of Aristo Toys created a sensation in the quiet market town of Mircester. A famous pop band called Children of the New Age performed on a platform outside the shop. A television detective, Buster Kemp, made a speech saying that it was important to buy good safe toys for children which could be passed down through the generations. 'Just think,' he said, holding up a doll, 'one of your grandchildren could be showing this in later years on *Antiques Roadshow*.'

Then the mayor cut the tape and the shop was declared open. May, dressed in a conservative suit and with her hair professionally dressed, was flanked by two assistants.

She could hardly believe that people were actually paying the extraordinarily steep prices Agatha had insisted on charging. Her toys had become a 'must have'.

'Thanks,' said Simon to Agatha when the long day was over. 'How will she restock?'

'I've leased a small factory on the outskirts. I've had May out there for the past three months training people. If you tap into the middle-aged and elderly workforce, it's amazing what talent you can find. I keep forgetting to ask May – did someone actually poison Carrie Brother's dog?'

'The vet said it died of old age and overeating. Carrie won't believe him. She's gone in for cats.'

Simon was leaving the shop when Toni caught up with him. 'Coming for a drink?'

'Sorry, Toni, I've got a date.'

'Oh, have fun.' Toni turned and walked away.

Simon swore under his breath. He could resign and then he'd be free to ask her out. But he loved the work.

Somehow, he would make Agatha Raisin so beholden to him that she would let him out of their agreement.

James Lacey studied the engagement columns in *The Times* but could not see any announcement of any engagement between Agatha and Charles. He had gone immediately off on his travels again after that scene in the kitchen.

But why should he mind so much? After all, it was he who had divorced Agatha. So why did the world suddenly seem such an empty place?

If you enjoyed *Agatha Raisin and the Busy Body*, read on for the first chapter of the next book in the *Agatha Raisin* series . . .

Agatha Raisin: As the Pig Turns

Chapter One

Agatha Raisin wearily turned on to the road leading down into her home village of Carsely in the Cotswolds and then came to an abrupt halt. Cars stretched out in front of her. She pulled on the handbrake.

It was the end of January and a very cold month, unusually cold. The tall trees on either side of the country road raised bare branches to a leaden sky as if pleading for the return of spring. Agatha prayed it would not snow. It seemed as if two centimetres of snow were enough to close down the roads, because the council complained they had run out of salt and all roads leading out of Carsely were very steep, making driving hazardous.

What on earth was going on? She gave an impatient blast on her horn, and the young man in the battered Ford in front gave her the finger.

Cursing, Agatha got out of her car and marched up to the Ford and rapped on the window. The sallow-faced youth opened the window and demanded, 'Wot?'

'What the hell's going on?' demanded Agatha.

The youth eyed her up and down, noting the expensively tailored coat and the beady, accusing eyes and marking the 'posh' accent. He scowled. 'Pot'oles,' he said with a shrug. 'They're repairing pot'oles.'

'And how long will it take?'

'Blessed if I know,' he said, and rolled up the window.

Agatha returned to the warmth of her car, fuming. She herself had complained bitterly to the council about the state of the road. But there were two other roads into the village. They might at least have put up diversion notices until the road was repaired. She contemplated making a U-turn but knew, considering her lack of driving skills, it would take her an awful lot of manoeuvring on the narrow road to do so.

A drip began to appear on the end of her nose. She reached into the box of tissues on the seat beside her and blew her nose. Someone rapped at the window.

Agatha looked out. A policeman was bending down looking at her. He was squat and burly, with a squashed-looking nose in his open-pored face and piggy, accusing little eyes.

Lowering the window, Agatha asked, 'How long is this going to take, Officer?'

'It'll take as long as it takes, madam,' he said in a thick Gloucestershire accent. 'I am ticketing you for taking your hands off the wheel.'

'My, what? Are you mad? I was simply blowing my nose. The handbrake's on, I'm stuck here . . .'

'Sixty-pound fine.'

'I'll see you in hell first before I pay that,' howled Agatha.

He handed in a ticket. 'See you in court.'

Agatha sat for a moment, shaking with rage. Then she took a deep breath. She started to negotiate a U-turn, but cars piled up behind her had decided to do the same thing. At last she was clear, just in time to see in her rear-view mirror that the line of cars she had just left had started to move.

By the time she reached her thatched cottage in Lilac Lane, it had begun to snow, fine little pellets of snow. Damn all pundits and their moaning about global warming, thought Agatha. As she opened the car door to get out, a gust of wind whipped the ticket the policeman had given her and sent it flying up over her cottage.

She let herself into her cottage. Her two cats, Hodge and Boswell, came running forward to give her the welcome they always gave when they wanted something to eat.

Agatha fed them, poured herself a gin and tonic, and then phoned her friend Detective Sergeant Bill Wong. When he came on the phone, Agatha complained bitterly about the policeman who had given her a ticket for blowing her nose.

'That would be Gary Beech,' said Bill, 'the target fiend. You know we have to meet certain targets or we don't get promotion. He goes a bit mad. The other week, a nine-year-old's mother who lives in a cul-de-sac in Mircester chalked squares on the pavement for her little boy to play hopscotch. Beech arrested the kid and charged him with the crime of graffiti. And he charged a toddler with carrying a dangerous weapon even though the kid was holding a water pistol. An old-age pensioner was arrested under the Terrorism Act for carrying a placard saying, "Get our boys out of Afghanistan".'

'What should I do?'

'It'll probably be thrown out of court. Or you could just pay the fine.'

'Never!'

'How's business?'

'Not good. The recession is really biting. People just don't have the money.' Agatha looked out of her kitchen window. 'Blast! The snow's getting thicker. I wish I'd invested in snow tyres or a four-wheel drive. Roy Silver's coming down for the weekend. I hope the roads clear by then.'

Roy had worked for Agatha when she had run a successful public relations business in London. She had taken early retirement and had sold up to move to the Cotswolds. But after solving several murders, she had decided to set up her own detective agency.

Bill said he would try to get down to see her at the weekend and rang off.

Agatha then phoned her agency. She had a small staff: Patrick Mulligan, a retired policeman, Phil Marshall, an elderly man from Carsely, young Toni Gilmour and a secretary, Mrs Freedman. A shrewd businesswoman, Agatha had seen the recession coming long before most people and so had decided not to employ any more staff. But there was one absence from her staff jabbing at her conscience. A bright young detective, Simon Black, employed by Agatha until a few months earlier, had shown signs of falling in love with Toni. Persuading herself that she was acting in their best interests, Agatha had told Simon that Toni was too young and to wait three years. But Toni had turned against Simon, feeling he was snubbing her at every turn, and to Agatha's horror, Simon had gone off and enlisted in the army and was now fighting in Afghanistan.

Toni answered the phone and said that Mrs Freedman and Phil had gone home, not wanting to wait any longer in case the snow got thicker. Toni, young, blonde and beautiful, often gave Agatha pangs of envy, but she had to admit that the girl was a brilliant detective.

'What have we got outstanding?' asked Agatha.

'Two adulteries, four missing pets and two missing teenagers.'

Agatha sighed. 'It seems not so long ago that I swore I would never take on another missing pet. Now we need the money.'

'It's easy money,' said Toni. 'They hardly ever think of checking the animal shelter. I just go along there with the photos they've given me of Tiddles or whatever, collect the beasts and phone the happy owners and then say, "Pay up".'

'Roy's coming down for the weekend,' said Agatha, 'and maybe Bill will come over. Why don't you join us and maybe I'll find something interesting for us to do?'

'I've got a date.'

'Who is he?'

'Paul Finlay.'

'How did you meet him?'

Toni longed to tell the ever-curious Agatha to mind her own business, but she said reluctantly, 'I've been taking French classes in the evenings, now that it's quiet at work. He's the lecturer.'

'How old is he?'

'I've got to go. The other phone's ringing.'

After she had rung off, Agatha sat and worried. Toni had a weakness for older men and had run into trouble before.

Agatha's cleaner, Doris Simpson, had left a local newspaper on the kitchen table. She began to search through it to see if there were any weekend amusements, and then her eye fell on an event in Winter Parva, a village some twenty miles away. Agatha had been to Winter Parva only once. It was a touristy Cotswold village with gift shops, a mediaeval market hall and thatched cottages. The article said that as the local shops had not fared as well as usual over the Christmas period, the parish council had planned to generate interest in the village with a special January event. There was to be a pig roast on Saturday on the village green. The villagers were urged to dress in old-fashioned costumes. The Winter Parva morris dancers would perform along with the local brass band and the village choir. Two busloads of Chinese tourists were expected to arrive for the event.

That'll do, thought Agatha, as long as I'm not blocked in the village by the snow.

Feeling hungry, she rummaged in her deep freezer to find something to microwave. Suddenly all the lights went out. A power cut.

She remembered the pub, the Red Lion, had a generator. Agatha changed into trousers, boots and a hooded parka and set out in the hunt for dinner.

The pub was crowded with locals. Agatha went to the bar and ordered lasagne and chips and a half of lager and looked around for a vacant table. Then, to her amazement, she saw her friend the vicar's wife, Mrs Bloxby, sitting by herself in a corner, looking down dismally at a small glass of sherry.

Agatha hurried to join her, wondering what could be wrong, because Mrs Bloxby never went to the pub unless it was some special fundraising occasion. The vicar's wife had grey hair escaping from an old-fashioned bun. Her normally kind face looked tired. She was wearing a shabby tweed coat over a washed-out sweater, cardigan and tweed skirt. It didn't matter what she wore, thought Agatha, not for the first time, Mrs Bloxby always had 'lady' stamped on her. Agatha and Mrs Bloxby always called each other by their second names, a tradition in the local Ladies' Society, of which both were members.

'How odd to see you here,' said Agatha. 'Where's your husband?'

'I neither know nor care,' said Mrs Bloxby. 'Do sit down, Mrs Raisin.'

Agatha sat down opposite her. 'What is the matter?'

Mrs Bloxby seemed to rally. She gave a weak smile. 'It's nothing, really. Do you really mean to eat that?'

The waitress had placed a dish of lasagne and chips in front of Agatha. 'Sure. What's up with it?' Agatha dug her fork in and took a mouthful.

Mrs Bloxby reflected that her friend had the taste buds of a vulture.

Yet Agatha sometimes managed to make her feel diminished. Although in her early fifties, Agatha glowed with health, and her glossy brown hair, although expertly dyed, gleamed like silk.

'It can't be nothing,' said Agatha, reaching for the ketchup bottle, opening it and dousing her chips.

'Probably my imagination,' said Mrs Bloxby wearily.

'You always did have good instincts. Out with it,' commanded Agatha.

Mrs Bloxby gave a heart-wrenching dry sob, the kind a child gives after crying for a long time. 'It's just that I think Alf is having an affair. You're dribbling ketchup.'

'Oh, sorry.' Agatha put a chip, overloaded with ketchup, back on her plate. 'Your husband is having an affair? Rubbish!'

'You're right. I'm just being silly.'

'No, no, I shouldn't have said that. I mean, who would want him?' remarked Agatha with her usual lack of tact.

Her friend bristled. 'I will have you know that as vicar of this parish, Alf has often been the target of predatory ladies.'

'So what makes you think he's having an affair? Lipstick on his dog collar?'

'Nothing like that. It's just that he's taken to sneaking off without his dog collar on and he won't tell me where he's going.'

'Been buying any new underwear recently?'

'No, I buy his underwear.'

'Look, I'll find out for you and put your mind at rest. On the house.'

'Oh, don't do that. If he saw you tailing him, he would be furious.'

'He won't see me. I happen to be a very good detective.'

'You are to do nothing about it,' said Mrs Bloxby seriously. 'Promise?'

'Promise,' agreed Agatha, and surreptitiously and childishly crossed her fingers behind her back.

A warm wind from the west during the night melted the snow to slush, and then, when the wind changed round to the north, it froze the roads into skating rinks. Agatha awoke the next day in a bad temper. How on earth was she going to get out of the village? It seemed small consolation that the power was back on.

But as she was having her usual breakfast of black coffee and cigarettes, she faintly heard a sound from the end of the lane, a sound she had not heard for some time. She put on her boots and coat and ran to the end of the lane. A gritter was making its lumbering way down through the village, spraying the road with grit and salt.

Agatha hurried back to put on her make-up and get dressed for the office.

She was just driving out of Lilac Lane when she recognized the vicar's car on the road ahead of her. 'Just a little look wouldn't hurt,' she assured herself. She let the car behind her pass her and then followed, keeping the vicar's car in view. He drove to the nearby village of Ancombe and parked in the courtyard of St Mary's, a large Catholic church. The village of Ancombe had remained loyal to Charles I when, all about, the Puritans supported Cromwell.

Driven by curiosity, Agatha parked out on the road and went up the drive past the gravestones and into the church.

In the dimness of the church, she could just make out the thin figure of Mr Bloxby going into a confessional box and closing the door. She ducked down in a pew as a priest appeared and went into the confessional.

I must know what he is saying, fretted Agatha. She took off her shoes and tiptoed towards the confessional box into which the vicar had disappeared, put her ear against it and listened hard.

'What do you think you are doing?' roared a stentorian voice.

Agatha caught a frightened glimpse of a man who had just entered the church. She quickly closed her eyes and slumped to the floor. The confessional opened and Mr Bloxby and the priest came out.

'What is going on?' demanded the reedy voice of the priest.

Agatha opened her eyes. 'What happened?' she demanded weakly. 'I felt dizzy and saw Mr Bloxby coming in here and wanted to ask him for help.'

'She was listening!' said a thin, acidulous man.

'I know this woman,' said Mr Bloxby. 'Mrs Raisin, step outside the church with me.'

Agatha got to her feet. No one helped her. She put on her shoes. Mr Bloxby marched ahead, and Agatha trailed after him, miserably.

Outside the church, Mr Bloxby snapped, 'Get in my car, Mrs Raisin. You have some explaining to do.'

Agatha got into the passenger seat of the vicar's car. It had begun to rain: soft, weeping rain.

'Now,' said Mr Bloxby, 'explain yourself, you horrible woman.' The vicar had never liked Agatha and could not understand his wife's affection for her.

She'll never speak to me again, thought Agatha sadly as she realized she would have to tell the truth.

'It's like this, Alf . . . may I call you Alf?'

'No.'

'Okay, what happened, I met your wife in the pub last night and she had been crying. She thinks you're having an affair.'

'How ridiculous . . . although come to think of it, I have had to ward off a few amorous parishioners over the years.'

'I promised not to snoop,' said Agatha.

'Which in your case is like promising not to breathe.'

'Right! I'm fed up feeling guilty,' said Agatha. 'What the hell were you doing in the confessional box of a Catholic church?'

'I needed spiritual guidance.'

'Don't tell me you've lost your faith?' demanded Agatha.

'Nothing like that. You know that we use the old Book of Common Prayer and the King James Bible?'

Agatha hadn't noticed, but she said, 'Yes.'

'It is the most beautiful writing, on a par with Shakespeare. The bishop has ordered me to change to modern translations of both. I can't, I just can't. I felt I had to unburden myself to a priest of a different faith.'

'Why on earth didn't you tell your wife?'

'I had to wrestle with my conscience. I even thought of entering the Catholic Church.'

'And taking a vow of celibacy?'

'The Vatican is proposing making provisions for people like myself.'

'Don't you *talk* to your wife?'

'I prefer to wrestle with spiritual matters on my own.'

Agatha saw a way out of her predicament. She threw him a cunning look out of her small, bearlike eyes. 'I could fix it for you.'

'You! Do me a favour.'

'I will, if you'll shut up and listen. The bishop will not go against the wishes of the parishioners. The whole village will sign a petition to keep things as they are and send it to the bishop. Easy. I'll fix it for you if you promise not to tell Mrs Bloxby I had anything to do with it. I'll fix it up with the local shop. Everyone shops there in the bad weather. I'll get Mrs Tutchell, the new owner, to say it's her idea. You start talking about it now, all round the village, starting with your wife. Of course, if I find you have breathed a word about my involvement in this, you're on your own, mate. Of all the silly vicars . . .'

'Why didn't you tell me before?' asked Mrs Bloxby plaintively half an hour later, after having heard her husband's explanation.

258

'At first, I wanted to wrestle with the problem on my own, but I called in at the village store and happened to mention it on my way home. The villagers have been very supportive and are sending a petition to the bishop.'

'Did Mrs Raisin have anything to do with this?'

'Of course not,' said the vicar, addressing the sitting-room fire. Just a white lie, God, he assured his Maker. 'Can you imagine me asking her for help?'

Agatha busied herself for most of the rest of the day by going door-to-door in the village, raising support for the vicar and urging everyone to sign the petition at the village store. A good proportion of the villagers were incomers who only went to church at Easter and Christmas but were anxious to do the right 'village thingie', as one overweight matron put it. Agatha headed to the office in the late afternoon to find Toni just leaving on the arm of a tall, tweedy man who sported a beard.

'This is Paul Finlay,' said Toni.

'Ah, the great detective,' said Paul. He was in his late thirties, Agatha guessed, with an infuriatingly patronizing air. He had a craggy face and the sort of twinkling humorous eyes that belie the fact that the owner has no sense of humour whatsoever.

'We're off out for the evening,' said Toni quickly. 'Bye.'

'Wait a bit,' said Agatha. 'Roy's coming on Friday night, and on Saturday we're going to a pig roast in Winter Parva. Why don't you and Paul come along?

Come to my cottage and I'll take you over because the parking's going to be awful.'

'A pig roast?' cackled Paul. 'How quaint. Of course we'll come.'

'Good. The pig roast starts at six, but I'd like to get there a bit earlier,' said Agatha. 'See you around four o'clock for drinks and then we'll all go.'

Agatha stood and watched them as they walked away. Toni's slim young figure looked dwarfed and vulnerable beside the tall figure of Paul.

'Not suitable at all. What a prick,' said Agatha, and a passing woman gave her a nervous look.

Agatha checked business in the office before heading home again. She was just approaching Lilac Lane when a police car swung in front of her, blocking her.

Agatha jammed on the brakes and looked through the window. She saw the lumbering figure of the policeman who had ticketed her for blowing her nose. She rolled down the window as he approached. 'Now what?' she demanded.

'I had a speed camera in me 'and up in that there road,' he said, 'and you was doing thirty-two miles an hour. So that's three points off your licence and a speed-ing fine.'

Agatha opened her mouth to blast him but quickly realized he would probably fine her for abusing a police officer. He proceeded to give her a lecture on the dangers of speeding, and Agatha knew he was trying to get her to lose her temper, so she listened quietly until he gave up.

When he had finally gone, she swung the car round and went into the village store, where she informed an interested audience about the iniquities of the police in general and one policeman in particular. 'I'd like to kill him,' she shouted. 'May he roast slowly over a spit in hell.'

It was a frosty Friday evening when Agatha met Roy Silver at Moreton-in-Marsh station. He was dressed in black trousers and a black sweater, over which he was wearing a scarlet jacket with little flecks of gold in the weave. He had shaved his head bald, and Agatha thought dismally that her friend looked like a cross between a plucked chicken and someone auditioning for a job as a Red Coat entertainer at a Butlin's holiday camp.

'Turn on the heater,' said Roy as he got in the car. 'I'm freezing.'

'I'm not surprised,' said Agatha. 'What's with the bald head?'

'It's fashionable,' said Roy petulantly, 'and it strengthens the hair. It's only temporary.'

'I'll lend you some warm clothes,' said Agatha.

'Your clothes on me, babes?' said Roy waspishly. 'I'd look as if I were wearing a tent. I mean, you could put two of me inside one of you.'

'I'm not fat,' snarled Agatha. 'You're unhealthily thin. Charles has left some of his clothes in the spare room.'

Sir Charles Fraith, a friend of Agatha's, often used her cottage as a hotel.

Roy said mutinously that his clothes were perfectly adequate, but when they got to Agatha's cottage, they found there had been another power cut and the house was cold.

While Agatha lit the fire in her living room, Roy hung away his precious jacket in the wardrobe in the spare room, wondering how anyone could not love such a creation. He found one of Charles's cashmere sweaters and put it on.

When he joined Agatha, the fire was blazing. 'How long do these power cuts last?' he asked.

'Not long, usually,' said Agatha. 'There's something up with the power station that serves this end of the village.'

'Anything planned for the weekend?'

'We're going to a pig roast at Winter Parva tomorrow.'

'No use. I'm vegetarian.'

'Since when?'

Roy looked shifty. 'A month ago.'

'You haven't been dieting. You've been starving yourself,' accused Agatha. 'I got steaks for dinner.'

'Couldn't touch one,' said Roy. 'A pig roast? Do you mean turned on a spit like in those historical films?'

'Yes.'

'Yuck, and double yucky, yucky yuck, Aggie. It'll be disgusting.'

But the next day after Toni and Paul had arrived, and the erratic electricity had come on again, Roy decided that anything would be better than being left behind. Bill Wong had phoned to say he could not make it.

Just as they were having drinks, Charles Fraith arrived. He was as expensively dressed as usual in smart casual clothes. He had small, neat features and well-barbered hair. Agatha never really knew what he thought of her. He helped himself to a whisky and then proceeded to put his foot in it. He asked Roy sympathetically if he had cancer. When Roy denied it, Charles said, 'I was about to forgive you for wearing one of my sweaters, but as you aren't suffering, I do feel you might have asked me first.'

'I told him he could borrow something,' said Agatha. 'I haven't introduced you to Paul Finlay.'

'Toni's uncle?'

'No, just a friend,' said Agatha.

Paul bristled. Charles's upper-class accent brought out the worst in him. His light Birmingham accent grew stronger as he suddenly treated them all to a rant about the unfairness of the British class system and about an aristocracy who lived on the backs of the poor.

Thank goodness for Charles, thought Agatha. Toni must see what a horror this man is.

But Toni was listening to Paul with shining eyes.

Charles waited until Paul had dried up, said calmly, 'What a lot of old-fashioned bollocks. When are we going?'

'Finish your drinks,' said Agatha. 'I want to be sure of getting a parking place. It'll be a bit of a crush in my car.'

'I'll take Roy,' said Charles.

'You'll need a coat,' said Agatha to Roy. 'You'll find my Barbour hanging in the hall. Use that.'

'I could wear my jacket,' said Roy.

'You'll freeze. Come along, everyone.'

Thin trails of fog wound their way through the trees as they drove to Winter Parva. They had to park outside the village because all the parking places in the village had been taken. Paul, anxious to get Toni to himself, said they would look at the shops and meet the others on the village green in time for the pig roast.

Agatha, Charles and Roy walked to the nearest pub and into the grateful warmth of the bar.

'Something will need to be done about Paul,' said Charles. 'I think Toni's still a virgin, and the thought of her losing it under the hairy thighs of that bore is horrible.'

'He might propose marriage,' said Roy.

'I think I'll do a bit of detective work,' said Agatha. 'I bet he's either married or been married. Why can't Toni see what a bore he is? How can she listen to that class nonsense?'

'Maybe it strikes a chord,' said Charles. 'You forget, she was brought up rough. Maybe she doesn't know where she belongs in the scheme of things. There can be something very seductive about that sort of propaganda. Where the hell did she meet him?'

'At evening classes in French,' said Agatha gloomily. 'He's the lecturer.'

Roy was looking round the bar at people dressed in mediaeval costume. 'We could have dressed up, Aggie,' he said plaintively.

Agatha looked at her watch. 'I think we'd better make our way to the village green. I want to see how they prepare this pig.'

The fog had thickened. If it hadn't been for the parked cars, you might have thought the village had reverted to the Middle Ages as the costumed villagers appeared and then disappeared in the fog.

Two men were bathing a huge pig in oil as it hung on a spit over a bed of blazing charcoal.

Some villagers were carrying flaming torches. As the fog lifted slightly, Agatha saw clearly on the haunch of the pig a tattoo of a heart with an arrow through it and the curly lettering 'Amy'. Her eyes flew down the length of the carcass to the chubby legs cut off above the knees.

'Stop!' she screamed at the top of her lungs.

The two men stopped turning the spit and stared at her. 'Pigs don't have tattoos,' said Agatha.

They peered at it. 'Reckon someone's been 'aving a bit o' a joke,' said one.

But Agatha had taken a powerful little torch out of her handbag and was examining the head.

'The head's been stitched on,' she said. 'Oh, God, I think this is the carcass of a man. Get the police.'

У.Н